Please to remember
The Fifth of November
Gunpowder, treason and plot.
I see no reason
Why gunpowder treason
Should ever be forgot.

Traditional rhyme

GUY FAWKES
from an engraving by George Cruikshank

(Courtesy Radio Times Hulton Library)

Gunpowder, Treason and Plot

by
Lettice Cooper
Illustrated by Elisabeth Grant

ABELARD – SCHUMAN

LONDON   NEW YORK   TORONTO

Library of Congress Catalogue Card No.70-120861
ISBN 0 200 71570 4

Printed in Great Britain by
Page Bros. (Norwich) Ltd.,
Norwich & London
Typesetting by Print Origination Liverpool

LONDON
Abelard-Schuman
Limited
8 King Street
W C.2

NEW YORK
Abelard-Schuman
Limited
257 Park Avenue South
N.Y.10010

TORONTO
Abelard-Schuman
Canada Limited
200 Yorkland Boulevard
425

Contents

			page
Chapter	1	A Conspiracy Begins	9
Chapter	2	The Return of Guy Fawkes	17
Chapter	3	The Oath	22
Chapter	4	Entry by Night	28
Chapter	5	The Conspiracy Grows	34
Chapter	6	The Vault	41
Chapter	7	A Time of Waiting	47
Chapter	8	The Thirteenth Conspirator	54
Chapter	9	The Unsigned Letter	60
Chapter	10	A Warning	67
Chapter	11	The King's Command	72
Chapter	12	A Second Warning	77
Chapter	13	The First Search	82
Chapter	14	Growing Suspicion	87
Chapter	15	Arrest	92
Chapter	16	The Second Search	96
Chapter	17	Bonfire Night	102
Chapter	18	The End of the Plot	108
Chapter	19	Trial and Punishment	115

For
Matthew Felix Cooper
to read later on

Author's Note

This book is an account of the Gunpowder Plot based on historical records. I have invented dialogue only where there are no historical records, and to bring the facts, all of which are true, to life.

L.C.

Chapter 1
A Conspiracy Begins

On a Spring morning in the year 1604 two young men met unexpectedly on the Westminster landing stage of the river Thames. Their names were Tom Winter and Jack Wright; they were distant cousins; they looked at one another and began to laugh.

"Tom! I might have known it."

"So Robin sent for you too?"

"Do you know what he wants us for?"

"He wrote only that he had urgent need of help in a great enterprise."

"He wrote the same to me."

"So we are here."

Of course we are here, they were both thinking. All their lives they had admired their brilliant cousin, Robert Catesby, and had followed his lead in any game he wanted to play.

"We had better take oars."

Tom Winter signalled to one of the wherries, the boats plying for hire on the water. The boat drew in to the landing stage, and the two young men stepped on board.

"Row us across, if you please, to a landing stage on the south bank. You will know the house because it stands directly opposite to the Parliament House."

They were carried out into the middle of the great river.

It was a busy thoroughfare on that fine Spring morning. A barge belonging to some nobleman swept by them, the eight oarsmen, in their livery of crimson and gold, swinging backwards and forwards together as their oars dipped and rose in unison. A swan moved with slightly ruffled dignity out of the wash from the barge. There were small wherries all over the water ferrying people from one landing stage to another. A coal barge, black as charred wood, made its slow way through the dense river traffic. Overhead the sun shone and the pale blue sky was lightly dappled with cloud.

The wherryman, thinking about his fee, noticed that the two young men, though gallant in their bearing, were not rich. Their doublets were rubbed by wear: they had no gold chains hanging below their ruffs, no jewels in the bands of their high-crowned hats. He guessed that they might be younger sons of some good but impoverished family. They might even, he thought, be Roman Catholics. Everyone knew that the Roman Catholics, who had been forced to pay heavy fines under Queen Elizabeth for adhering to their faith, were still having to pay them under King James I, who had now been a year on the throne of England.

The wherry cut across the main stream of traffic and drew near to the Lambeth bank.

"That will be it," Jack Wright pointed to a shabby-looking house standing alone on the marshy shore.

"What possessed Robin to come and live in such a desolate, aguish place?"

"Perhaps he could afford no other."

Tom Winter nodded. "Most likely."

The wherryman had been right. The cousins were Catholics who had already paid heavy fines, but so far had been lucky enough to escape imprisonment.

The wherry nosed in along the reeds and bumped against the rotting planks of an old landing stage.

"This must be it, for it is the only dwelling on this bank opposite to Parliament House."

"And there is Robin coming to meet us."

They paid the wherryman, ran up the short flight of dilapidated wooden steps, and threw themselves into the arms of a tall, dark-haired, remarkably handsome young man who came quickly to them with his own arms outstretched.

"Tom! Jack!"

"Robin!"

"I knew you would come. It's good to see you both."

"What's in the wind, Robin?"

"Come into the house and I will tell you."

With an arm through one of each, laughing, turning his head from one to the other, he led them indoors. Tom Winter and Jack Wright felt their spirits rise. From the time when they were all boys playing together in the country, the mere sight of Robin had always made life more interesting.

Robert Catesby took them to an upstairs room with a window that looked out over the river. He called to his servant, Thomas Bates, to bring a flagon of wine.

When Bates had gone out, Tom Winter, with a full glass of wine in his hand, strolled to the window.

"You choose a strange dwelling, Robin! You cannot look out across the river without seeing the accursed Parliament House where these cruel laws are made to oppress Catholics."

Robert Catesby had flung himself into a chair, his handsome head tilted back. He too had paid heavy fines, but he always managed to make himself look splendid. His ruby, quilted doublet glowed freshly and his ruff was edged with tiny pearls.

"Do you think it so strange that I should choose to live opposite Parliament House? The cat crouches opposite the mousehole until the time comes to spring."

He had spoken with so much meaning that the two cousins stared at him.

"What do you mean, Robin?"

"That I took this house for a purpose. As I asked you both to come here for a purpose."

"What purpose?"

Catesby replied calmly. "My purpose is to blow up the Parliament House with gunpowder on the day of the Opening of Parliament. King James will be there—King James who promised more tolerance for Catholics and then betrayed us. The Queen will be there and the young Prince Henry; and the Chief Minister, Cecil, that little grey beagle who hunts us down without mercy ... and the other Ministers and Lords and Commons who plan to make more laws to persecute us for adhering to our faith. With one swift secret stroke we shall send them all to their death. Then the country will be in our hands."

There was a silence of sheer astonishment.

"Are you mad, Robin?"

"No."

"It would be impossible."

"No."

Catesby smiled at their astounded faces.

"No, it would not be impossible, only difficult. We would store gunpowder here in this house, and ferry it over secretly by night to the other side. We should hire some house close to the Parliament House and dig a tunnel underground to the cellars below Parliament House, and pack the cellar with gunpowder and lay a mine with a fuse and a slow match. It has often been done by soldiers besieging a walled town. A skilled engineer trained in the foreign wars could do it."

"But . . . but we are not skilled engineers."

"We should find one. I know the right man for the work."

Tom Winter was still staring as if he did not believe that Robin could mean what he was saying.

Jack Wright said earnestly, "If it is possible to attempt such a thing have you thought that if we should make the attempt and fail we should not be the only ones who would suffer? Every Catholic in this country would be worse treated because of this attempt."

"Could we be worse treated than we are now? Think of the priests creeping from hiding hole to hiding hole after dark, and saying Mass only at the risk of their lives. Think how we are all watched and spied upon, and may find ourselves any day hauled before the courts for no crime but worshipping God in the way we choose. Think how clipped and confined we are. You, Tom, you are a man of capacity, you speak French, Latin, Spanish and Italian with ease, but what hope have you or any other promising young Catholic of a good post in the service of your country? There is no future for you but to live on what is left of your estate here until even that is taken away from you, or to go and fight for Spain in Flanders, as Guy Fawkes has done."

"Guy Fawkes?" Jack Wright exclaimed. "Guy Fawkes of York? Why I was at school with him. I did not know he had gone to fight in the foreign wars. I have not heard of him for several years."

"But I have," Tom Winter struck in. "He went with me last year on a mission to the King of Spain to beg him to find some way of helping English Catholics. But it was soon clear to us that his Spanish Majesty did not mean to lift a finger for us."

"I can tell you two important things about Guy Fawkes," Catesby said. "He is a skilled military engineer, and he has been abroad for so long that he is forgotten in England. His face would not be known here; he is not marked down as a Catholic like the rest of us by Cecil's spies."

There was a long silence. Then Tom Winter said, "I see, Robin, that you are serious in this purpose."

Robert Catesby jerked forward the hilt of his sword. It was engraved with a representation of the crucifixion of Christ. He laid his hand on the engraving.

"I have lost untimely my father, my wife and my son. Since I have twice been fined heavily for being a Catholic, I have been driven to sell the greater part of my estates. I cannot hope for any advancement at court, nor am I likely to be allowed to rise in any worthwhile profession. I have nothing left but my faith. I am ready to die for it."

Jack Wright said doubtfully, "If we blow up the King, the Lords and Commons, will there not be chaos in the country?"

"We shall take the young Princess Elizabeth and bring her up to be a Catholic Queen."

Catesby looked at his cousins. He was smiling, daring them as he had dared them long ago when he wanted them to help him to take an unbroken colt and ride him. "Jack? Tom? Are you with me?"

"I am with you, Robin," Jack said.

"Are you, Tom?"

"I would ask one thing," Tom said slowly. "A Spanish Embassy led by the Constable of Castile is to visit King James this summer. Let us go to the Constable and beg him to influence the King to abate the penalties for his English subjects. It would be a terrible thing to send so

15

many men to sudden death by gunpowder. Let us make this one more attempt to help ourselves by peaceful means. It if fails then I, too, am with you."

Catesby's smile was twisted and a little scornful; he had no hopes of the mission to the Constable, and he did not really expect his cousin to make conditions before falling in with his plans. But he saw that Tom Winter was determined.

"As you will, Tom. Go yourself to the Constable of Castile and try to persuade him. If he will not agree to do anything for us, then come back to England by way of the Low Countries and bring Guy Fawkes with you. I have been making inquiries about him lately. I know that he is a man of the most resolute courage and devoted to the Catholic faith."

Catesby picked up the flagon of wine, and filled all three glasses.

"Tom! Jack! My very dear cousins and oldest friends! I give you a toast. To the Gunpowder Plot! Destruction to King, Lords and Commons, and a Catholic England again!"

Chapter 2
The Return of Guy Fawkes

A few weeks later, a ship from Gravelines in the Low Countries sailed up the Thames Estuary and docked at Greenwich.

"We must take oars now, Guy," Tom Winter said.

Guy Fawkes nodded. It was strange to him to be called Guy again. He had for so long been Guido Fawkes, an English captain in the Spanish army.

There were plenty of wherry boats waiting near the dock to take off passengers from the big seagoing ships. Soon a couple of stout oarsmen were rowing Tom Winter and Guy Fawkes up the great river towards the heart of London.

Guy Fawkes looked eagerly about him. He was thirty four years old, and he had left his own country when he was twenty one. This was the first time he had returned to it. He had not expected to come back at all while the laws against Catholics were so strict, but he had felt it to be his duty, as soon as he learned that he was urgently needed, to do some special service for his religion. What that service was he did not yet know.

Tom Winter looked closely at Guy Fawkes as they were rowed up the river. Ever since they had met in Brussels, Winter had wondered whether this soldier of fortune would fall in with Robert Catesby's plan. Once again Tom

Winter scrutinized his companion; his eyes travelled from the reddish hair and the thin, bearded face down the long, lean body. Guy Fawkes had fought hard and lived without comforts; he looked older than his years. He struck Tom Winter as being a man of great determination. He was not easy company, he talked and smiled very little; he seemed to be a serious man, one who did not care for pleasure but was intent only on his religion and on soldiering. No doubt risking his life was an everyday hazard to him. Yes, probably Robin has been right, as he so often was, this would be the very man for his purpose.

The wherry drew level with the Tower of London, that great walled fortress on the bank of the river where so many people had been imprisoned only to walk out to their execution.

Tom Winter, thinking of this, said, "Sir Walter Raleigh, whom King James suspects of treachery to him, is now imprisoned in the Tower, and it is said that he may never come out except to lose his head on Tower Hill."

"Very likely," Guy Fawkes replied without much interest. Tom Winter had discovered that there were many things in which Guy was not interested, perhaps because he felt so strongly about the things that did matter to him.

Now the wherry was passing under London Bridge, that street crowded with shops and dwelling houses which spanned the water on its nine great arches. The spire of the old St. Paul's Church soared up on their right above a jumble of roof tops. They were passing the homes built by noble families on the North bank; their gardens sloping down to the river were full of green grass and bright flowers. Ahead were the Towers of Westminister Abbey, and the new royal Palace of Whitehall with the Parliament House between them.

The wind blew fresh and cool off the water. Guy

Fawkes wrapped his cloak round himself, and clapped a hand to the brim of his tall hat. What was he thinking about, Tom Winter wondered.

Fawkes, who was more moved by returning to his own country than he cared to show, was remembering his early life in the Northern city of York. His father had belonged to the Church of England. He had been a notary of the Ecclesiastical Court, and he and his wife and little son had always been about York Minster, the great Cathedral whose grey walls and towers rose up like a sudden miracle out of the narrow streets of the city.

King Henry VIII was right, Guy's father said, to throw off allegiance to the Pope, and give England a Church of her own, even if he did it because the Pope would not allow him to divorce Queen Catherine and marry Anne Boleyn. Queen Elizabeth was right when she kept a firm hand on the Catholics, and had Mary Queen of Scots executed when the Spanish Armada was coming so that she might not be used as a tool of Philip of Spain.

But Guy Fawkes was only eight years old when his father died. His mother soon married again. This time she married a Catholic. Now young Guy heard the other side of the story. King Henry VIII was wrong, his stepfather said, to cause the Church of England to break away from the Catholic Church which alone had divine authority. Queen Elizabeth was wrong to oppress Catholics, and it was wrong to execute Mary Queen of Scots, who was a martyr to the true faith.

Guy was very young and his stepfather was very kind. His mother became a Catholic, and almost without knowing it he found himself changing his faith as she did. He was baptized into the Catholic Church.

This meant that in England a great many professions were closed to him, and if he was caught hearing Mass, he

was liable for fines or imprisonment. He went abroad and enlisted in the Spanish army fighting in the Netherlands. He did not allow himself to see that the Netherlands had a just cause and that the Spaniards were invading and cruelly ill-treating a free people. He only cared that he was fighting for people of the same religion as his own.

As they drew near to the Parliament House, Tom Winter said, "You are so lucky that you are not known to Cecil's spies. The rest of us never know when we may be picked up and dragged off to prison."

"It is no better under King James?"

"It is worse, for all he promised to change things for us."

Guy Fawkes did not answer. He thought, "Whatever my religion needs from me here, that I must do."

The wherry shot across the river under the bows of a City Alderman's stately barge. As the oars nearly touched him, an indignant swan flew up, spreading his great wing span between the sunshine and the water. The wherry, slipping in front of a barge loaded with timber, was soon nosing in among the reeds and marsh marigolds on the South bank of the river. One of the oarsmen reached out with a boathook, and drew the wherry into the landing stage in front of Catesby's house.

Chapter 3
The Oath

One evening, in the following week, Guy Fawkes was walking at dusk through the streets of London. He was on his way to a house behind St. Clement's Inn, near to St. Clement's Church in the Fields.

He did not yet know what he had been summoned to England for. He knew that for several days Robert Catesby had been watching him and testing him for some secret purpose. He sometimes smiled sardonically, knowing well that he had carried out enterprises and encountered risks such as this fine young gentleman, flaunting about in his scarlet doublets and his jewelled hat bands, had never heard of.

All the others knew the secret. Tom Winter, and Jack Wright with whom Guy Fawkes has been at school in York, and another Yorkshireman, Thomas Percy, who was cousin to the Earl of Northumberland. Tom Percy was older than the rest of them, a red-faced, white-haired swashbuckler of nearly fifty, who in his youth had often picked a quarrel for the sheer pleasure of fighting. Before King James came down to England to sit upon the throne, Tom Percy had ridden up to Scotland to beg him to show mercy to Catholics during his reign. James had promised to do so and had already broken his promises. Tom Percy regarded this, as he had regarded so many things in his stormy life, as a personal insult. He was furious with the King.

"If they do not tell me their secret tonight," Guy Fawkes muttered to himself, "I shall go back to Flanders."

All he knew about the plan for the evening was that a priest would be there to say Mass. For any Catholic priest caught celebrating Mass in England the penalty was death, so it was not surprising that they should have to meet in this out-of-the-way part of London after dark.

When Guy Fawkes reached the house, the other four were already there, in a state of suppressed excitement.

Catesby held a Missal, the Catholic prayer book, in his long thin hands. He put it down on a table. "Gentlemen," he said. "Before I reveal what I have to tell tonight, let us all swear an oath of secrecy. Let us lay our hands upon this book. You will swear by the Blessed Trinity, and by the Sacrament you are now to receive, never to disclose directly or indirectly by word or circumstance the matter that shall be proposed to you to keep secret, nor to desist from the executing thereof until the rest shall give you leave."

In turn Guy Fawkes, Tom Percy, Tom Winter and Jack Wright each laid a hand upon the Missal, and swore as Robin Catesby had told them to do. He himself took the oath last. Then they all went into another room. Altar vessels and a small silver crucifix stood upon a table which had been covered with an embroidered cloth. Father Gerard waited by this temporary altar. He was a priest of the Jesuit order, who had already been imprisoned and tortured in the Tower of London, but has escaped by climbing down a rope into the moat. He still risked his life constantly by carrying out his priestly offices wherever they were wanted.

He said Mass now and gave the sacrament to the five

men. He had not been informed why they wanted to receive it together, and as soon as the service was over, he left the house and slipped away into the dark. It was safer for him to know nothing of Catesby's plan, and safer for any priest if even faithful Catholics did not know his next hiding place.

As soon as he had gone, Robin Catesby told the others of his plan to blow up the King, Lords and Commons in the Parliament on the opening day.

Guy Fawkes had no scruples about joining in the plot. He thought that the situation of Catholics was so desperate that a desperate remedy was needed. All the young men managed somehow to separate being Catholics in their minds from behaving like Christians.

Guy Fawkes considered the practical problems of the scheme. "It could be done," he said, "provided that we can get possession of a house near enough to Parliament House so that we can tunnel through and lay a mine underneath it."

Catesby nodded. "I had thought of that. I have been looking around and making inquiries. There is a house just right for our purpose. Its wall adjoins the wall of Parliament House. It belongs to Master Whyniard, the Keeper of the King's Wardrobe, but he does not use it himself. It is let to a Master Ferris."

"Then how are we to get possession of it?"

"You must do that, Percy. Your Cousin of Northumberland is powerful at court. You must persuade your cousin that you need this house for yourself and that no other will do. The Earl must speak to Whyniard to turn this Ferris out and let the house to you."

"But I cannot live there. Everyone knows that I am agent for my cousin in Northumberland, that I am almost always with him in his house, and have to ride North to his estates on business for him. How can I suddenly go and live in another house away from my cousin? Besides, I have never made any secret of my religion. If I move to a house near the Parliament House, Cecil's spies are likely to keep a watch on it, and perhaps search it."

"Of course you cannot live there," Catesby agreed. "None of us who are known to the Government spies must ever be seen crossing the threshold. The house will be occupied for the time being by your servant, John Johnson, a very honest, decent man whose face has hardly ever been seen in London, certainly not for a dozen years. A quiet, soberly dressed man like John Johnson can live in your house as caretaker and go in and out about his ordinary business without attracting notice."

Thomas Percy looked puzzled. "But I have no such servant. I know no John Johnson."

"Not by that name perhaps," Catesby said smiling. "But you do know him. As soon as you have got possession of the house you will give him the keys and he will be in charge of the whole place from attic to cellar. Especially the cellar. Have I said right, Fawkes? Are you willing to play the part of John Johnson?"

Guy Fawkes considered for a minute, frowning thoughtfully. "Yes," he said, "I will do it."

Catesby nodded as if he had expected no other answer. "So do you, Tom Percy, arrange as soon as you can to rent Whyniard's house. If the present tenant's lease is still running, your cousin the Earl must use his influence to have him put out before his time."

"Have you been inside this house?" Guy Fawkes asked.

"No, but I have been all around the outside very carefully at night after dark when there was such a storm of rain and wind that no one was likely to hear me."

"Is the cellar wall of stone?"

"I think so."

"Then if Parliament is to reopen in February of next
year we must begin our tunnelling this autumn. Meanwhile
we have to lay in a good store of gunpowder."

"I had that in mind," Catesby said, "when I rented my
house on the opposite bank. It is lonely there among the
marshes, few people come except those who come to see
me. We can store the gunpowder there and when we have
Whyniard's house we can ferry it across the river by night,
a barrel or two at a time. In the same way we can take in
tools, and anything else we need."

Catesby stood up and flung his heavy crimson cloak
round his shoulders. "We must not all leave this house at
the same time. But gentlemen, before we separate, I must
remind you that to blow up Parliament House with
everyone in it can only be part of our design. We must stir

26

up Catholics all over the country to be ready for great events. It will not be enough to dispose of the King and his heir. If we are to establish a Catholic rule in England we must make preparations so that the sudden blow will be followed by a general uprising."

Chapter 4
Entry by Night

On a dark night of December of the same year, 1604, a boat was moored at the landing stage below Robert Catesby's house. His servant, Thomas Bates, kneeling on a plank that he had laid across the marshy ground, was tying pieces of sacking round the blades of the oars so that they would only make a muffled noise as they struck the water.

Through the noise of the rain and the slapping of water against the boat he heard footsteps on the rickety stairs that led up to the house.

"Tom!"

"I am here, Sir. I have just finished muffling the oars."

Catesby, with Tom Winter and Jack Wright, and another young man called Robert Keyes, came down to the landing stage. They moved cautiously on the steps, as each one was heavily laden. Keyes was one of the household of a Catholic peer, Lord Mordaunt, who lived in Bedfordshire. He was a close friend of Catesby's and had been asked to join the band because they needed another man to collect and guard the necessary stores in Robert Catesby's house while he and his cousin rode about the country stirring up their Catholic friends to be ready for an uprising.

"I will get in," Catesby said. "You hand the packages to me. I will stow them safely on board." He stepped down into the boat and held out his arms. "The tools first."

The other young men put into his arms several bundles of tools carefully sewn up in sacking, not only to keep out the damp, but to make sure that there would be no clink of metal in case anyone should be about when they were unloaded at the other side of the river.

"Now the food."

Bags of flour and salt, a cold capon, cooked by Thomas Bates, and wrapped in a linen cloth, a small keg of ale, a barrel of salt fish, a package of dried herbs, a box of apples. Catesby took them all and stowed them away in the boat.

"Now, Tom, Jack, in with you."

As Tom Winter settled to his oar, the keg of ale rolled against his leg. He kicked it away.

"A pox on it, Robin! You have provisioned us for a siege. Was it necessary to take all this food?"

"We must do nothing to draw attention to the house. It is so near the Parliament House that the least thing might cause Cecil's spies to search it. If John Johnson, living alone there as caretaker, were suddenly to buy food for four people in the shops it could be enough to cause talk."

"You are right, Robin." It had always been the same. When they played games together as boys, Robin had thought of possibilities that would never have occurred to Tom and Jack.

Robert Catesby called softly to Keyes and Tom Bates. "One of us will slip across at night before Christmas. If you have any urgent need to speak to me hang a carpet out of my bedroom window in the morning and I will come. God be with you."

Almost without a sound the boat vanished into the rain and the dark.

Thomas Bates shook his head doubtfully as he walked back with Keyes to Catesby's house. He had not been told what the plan was, but he guessed enough to make him very anxious. He was devoted to his master.

In the boat there was silence for a few minutes as the muffled oars dipped and rose. The water was choppy, rocking the boat. The rain beat down upon their heads. To keep up his spirits Tom Winter began to whistle the tune of a Christmas carol.

"Only ten days till Christmas," Catesby muttered, "and till the Opening of Parliament on February 7th only another six weeks. We have so much to do in the time."

As they came near to the Westminster bank, they could just discern the dark shape of the Parliament House. They rowed past it. The house that Tom Percy had managed to rent from Whyniard stood next to the Parliament House. It had a long narrow slip of garden running down to the river bank. It was a small house with only one room upstairs, one on the ground floor, and the cellar below on which their hopes were set. There was no landing stage, but the supposed caretaker, John Johnson, who of course was really Guy Fawkes, had been laying down some planks, and had driven in a pole and fixed a staple with a chain so that it was possible to moor a boat.

He was there now on the bank, carrying a horn lantern with one shutter closed and the other half open so that it shed a pale gleam of light to guide them to his makeshift landing stage. They heard his deep voice on the bank above them.

"A yard further on. All is quiet above at the house. All is well. Hand me the supplies."

"Take the tools first." Catesby handed up the precious bundles.

Guy Fawkes grasped them. Yes, these were the things that mattered, more than any supply of food, more perhaps than the eager young men in the boat. If he had

the tools, Fawkes thought, he might be able to manage
almost as well without the others. There were moments
when he felt that they were like boys playing a game,
whereas he was an experienced soldier conducting a
military operation.

Next morning, when they began to try to make a tunnel

through the cellar walls, it irked him that he so often had to leave them. John Johnson, the caretaker, was the only one of the party who dared show himself. He had to answer if anyone knocked at the door of the house. People sometimes came to ask for Ferris, whose lease had been so ruthlessly cut short so that the Earl of Northumberland's cousin, Tom Percy, could have the house when he wanted it. Besides, John Johnson had to go about and do his shopping as usual; he had to show himself at the door or window; it would not be wise to let people think that the house was empty. John Johnson acted as sentry and look-out man all day, while the other three struggled, with more energy than experience, to make a tunnel. After dark, John Johnson could help them and could do his share of the tiresome job of carrying out the buckets of rubble that they had dislodged and burying them in the garden.

Tom Percy, as the present tenant of the house, was also free to come in and out, when he could do so without attracting notice. He slipped in whenever he could to lend a hand with the work, or to set Guy Fawkes free from keeping watch.

Robert Catesby and his two cousins had never done such difficult work in their lives. They did not know how to do it, and although Guy Fawkes was well able to show them he could not in a few days make them as expert with the pick as they were with the swords and horses they had grown up with. But they stuck to it, fired by their burning sense of the injustice done to Catholics and by their determination to change it.

Catesby often wondered, as he tried to swing his pick in a cramped space, how the preparations for the uprising in the country were going on. Had the Catholics whom he had visited begun to buy horses? Had they laid in any store of powder? Had they alerted other people who could be trusted and arranged a signal? How far would they be ready by February 7th? At other times Catesby wondered gloomily if the tunnel would be ready by then.

Christmas Eve was a day of triumph. They had, at last, broken through the cellar wall, and reached the foundation wall of Parliament House. True, they would have to tunnel through that, and it was of stone and reputed to be nine feet thick. But at least they had come to the end of the first stage, and sometimes it had seemed to them that they never would, so they were greatly encouraged. They carefully set props of wood, the way Fawkes had shown them, to hold up the last foot of their tunnel, and then crawled back into the cellar and climbed the stairs to the ground-floor room, stamping their cold feet and swinging their cramped arms.

Guy Fawkes was out shopping. He had gone to buy as much extra food as he thought wise so that they could have a Christmas meal.

He opened the front door and came in laden with bundles.

Robert Catesby cried out triumphantly, "We are through the cellar wall. We can touch the foundation wall of Parliament House with our tools."

Then he stopped short for he felt that something was wrong. Guy Fawkes lowered his armful of bundles onto the table.

"I have just seen a new proclamation about the date of the Opening of Parliament. It is postponed, from February 7th next year to October 3rd."

Chapter 5
The Conspiracy Grows

In the Palace of Whitehall, only a few hundred yards from the house where the conspirators were digging their tunnel, King James and his court celebrated Christmas with all the traditional rejoicings.

The King, who had come from the poor country of Scotland, was delighted to find himself so much richer as King of England. This Christmas he poured out extravagant presents on his three children, Prince Henry who was nine years old, Princess Elizabeth who was eight, and Prince Charles, a delicate child of four, who was, though nobody then expected it, to come to the throne next as Charles I.

The Queen, who had been Princess Anne of Denmark, loved dressing up and acting and dancing. She particularly wished to appear in a masque, a performance which included acting, singing and dancing. The poet Ben Jonson and the architect Inigo Jones combined this Christmas to compose a masque for her. The Queen and her ladies wore dresses stitched with gold, and spangled with jewels. The whole court wore new rich clothes and feasted and danced and sang all night.

In and out of this magnificence but indifferent to it, went Cecil, the King's chief Minister, a small, pale, hunchbacked man, always intent on the business of the realm. He had been chief Minister to Queen Elizabeth in the last years of her reign, as his father had been through all the early part of it. Because Cecil was very small, King James nicknamed him "the little beagle." The little beagle had inherited from his father an all-absorbing care for the welfare of the country and a deep distrust of Catholics, who, to his mind, were always likely to cause trouble and to act inside the country as secret allies of hostile foreign powers.

The conspirators in Whyniard's house did not spend a cheerful Christmas. Since none of them except the supposed John Johnson dared to show themselves outside they had no opportunity of hearing Mass. Catesby, his two cousins and Tom Percy were beginning to realize that it was going to be very difficult to tunnel through a nine-foot stone wall even though there would be so much more time than they had expected before the opening of Parliament.

In other ways, this added to their difficulties. Owing to the heavy fines imposed on Catholics, all the young men were poor; Guy Fawkes had lived for years on his soldier's pay and he was not now earning it. All of them were short of money to live on and they needed extra money to buy gunpowder with; they would need arms and horses for the uprising which they hoped to organize in the Midlands. They decided to invite two other men to join them, Jack Wright's younger brother, Christopher or Kit, and Tom Winter's elder brother, Robert.

Robert, although a devout Catholic, had been luckier than the others. He had not been fined or imprisoned; he lived quietly in his beautiful house at Huddington in Worcestershire where he had a secret chapel in which Mass was often celebrated. He had guessed from his brother Tom's obvious preoccupation that something was going on. When Catesby and Tom told him what they proposed to do, Robert allowed himself to be drawn into the plot by family feeling and because of his religion, but he was never quite easy in his mind about the terrible destruction that they were planning.

Kit Wright was a young daredevil who joined the Earl of Essex in his revolt against Queen Elizabeth just before the end of her reign. He had been imprisoned and fined as a punishment, and he was as poor as the other young men. Only Robert Winter was able to contribute a substantial sum of money to the enterprise.

These two new recruits joined the other conspirators in Whyniard's house, and helped with the hard, slow work on the tunnel. With Robert Winter's money they bought gunpowder and stored it in Catesby's house across the river.

They also supplied themselves with guns and plenty of ammunition. They were all determined, if they were surprised at their tunnelling, to die fighting. But no one thought of examining the narrow slip of a house next to the Parliament House.

On February 10th, the King made a long speech in the Council Chamber. He declared that any Papists who hoped that he would tolerate the practice of their religion would be disappointed. He had never intended to make things easier for them, and if he thought his sons would be more lenient to Catholics than he was, he would disinherit them and make his daughter his heir. He would strengthen the laws against Catholics, and insist that they should be applied without mercy.

This speech, which most people thought had been inspired by Cecil, made the young men in the cellar of Whyniard's house work even harder. Each night after dark they carried out buckets full of rubble from the hole they were making and buried the stuff in the garden.

While they were eating or resting, Catesby, who was the real organizer of the plot, explained his plans to the others.

"Prince Henry, being the heir to the throne, will attend the Opening of Parliament with his father and mother, so he will be blown up too."

Robert Winter looked unhappy and said that the boy was very young.

"He is forward for his age, and already a staunch Protestant. They would rally to him, he is much loved. No, we must make Princess Elizabeth our Queen, and bring her up in the Catholic faith."

"And the young Prince Charles?"

"We must take possession of him, too. But he is such a weak and sickly child that it is unlikely that he will live much longer. He cannot yet walk at four years old."

"The Princess Elizabeth lives most of the year at Combe Abbey in Warwickshire, in the care of her governess, Lady Hartington. I shall arrange a hunting party on the day after the Opening of Parliament and shall invite all the Catholic gentlemen of good faith in the area. We shall seize the Princess and raise the standard of revolt. If we need to establish ourselves in a fortress, there is John Grant's house at Norbrook which is well defended by wall and moat. Grant will do anything for our cause. He has taken the oath of secrecy and joins us."

"So now we are nine," Tom Winter said.

"No, ten," Catesby answered. "I have lately observed my servant, Tom Bates, looking at me most strangely. I asked him what ailed him. He said that he felt sure that I was about some dangerous business, and that it was connected with Whyniard's house and Parliament House. Since he was so near the mark, I thought it safest to tell him the truth. He took the oath of secrecy on the Missal. He is a good honest fellow, devoted to me. We are

37

perfectly safe in trusting him. So, now, let us work again
at the tunnel for it is clear that the fate of every Catholic
in England hangs upon these few square feet of stone
wall."

The young men took up their picks again. They worked
in shifts all day and took turns to bury the rubble at night.
Only John Johnson ever went out by the front door of the
house to buy food or anything else they needed, and to
bring back news. One night, Tom Bates rowed over after
dark from Catesby's house, and brought them a few barrels
of gunpowder. The young men lived like moles burrowing
in the dark. Only Guy Fawkes knew, and Catesby was
beginning to suspect, what little progress they had made

through the nine-foot wall of solid stone.

Then, one day, when they were working doggedly in the hole they heard an extraordinary sound ahead of them. It was a rattling, rushing noise, as if a great piece of the wall were falling.

The conspirators were startled. Could it be that all their chipping and hammering had dislodged some stones on the other side where they hoped to break through? If so, their attempt was bound to be discovered. The young men hastily lowered their tools and crawled out of the hole to wait until Guy Fawkes went to try and find out what had happened.

He came back an hour or two later. He was not a man whose face ever showed much expression, it was always hard to judge if anything surprised or excited him, but this time the others saw at once that he had something important to tell them. They crowded round him.

"What news, Guy? What news?"

"The best of news. It may be we can put away our picks. There is a cellar to let under Parliament House. It belongs to a vendor of coal, Andrew Bright, who is moving his stock to a larger and more convenient place. The noise that you heard was the fall of coal as his present stock was being moved out. If we can rent the cellar, we shall need no tunnel. We can store our gunpowder there under piles of ordinary firewood, and we shall be able to lay our mine immediately below the floor of Parliament House. I hear that Bright is away in Yorkshire arranging for shipments of coal, but his wife, Ellen, has the keys of the cellar. We should see her at once."

"You, Tom Percy," Catesby exclaimed. "You have the lease of this house. You must see Mrs. Bright and tell her that you have a lot of furniture and other goods stored in this cellar and that you need another cellar for fuel.

Do not offer her too high a price so as to make her suspicious, but make sure of getting the cellar whatever bargain you have to strike with her. We will find the money somehow. And tell Mrs. Bright that your servant, John Johnson, who is the caretaker of this house, and a most honest, trustworthy fellow who has been in your service for years, will keep the keys of her cellar, and look after everything there."

Tom Percy was successful. On March 25th of that year, 1605, Mrs. Ellen Bright gave him the lease of the cellar under Parliament House, for which Percy agreed to pay a rent of five pounds a year.

The plotters felt that Heaven was on their side. Now they need no longer lie hidden in Whyniard's house; there was no back-breaking work to do in cramped positions, no more creeping out at night with heavy sacks of rubble.

All the conspirators would have to do now would be to fill the cellar under Parliament House with gunpowder, to prepare a Catholic uprising in the country, and to keep the secret until the Opening of Parliament on October 3rd.

Chapter 6
The Vault

The cellar was just what they needed. Right underneath the Great Hall of Parliament House, it was seventy feet long and twentyfour feet wide. It was vaulted, there was plenty of room for storage, and it was so damp and dark that nobody was likely to be interested in it for any other purpose.

The conspirators already had twenty barrels of gunpowder hidden in Catesby's house across the river. They ferried these over, a few at a time, by night and stored them in Whyniard's house. On a wet, dark night when the streets were empty they rolled them into the vault and covered them with stones and iron bars.

The supposed John Johnson ordered three thousand logs of wood to be delivered to the cellar entrance. Master Percy, he remarked to the man who sold the wood, needed a great deal of fuel; belonging as he did to a noble family, he had many valuable pieces of furniture, and tapestries and hangings. He kept the best of these in Whyniard's house, and he was anxious to keep the house well-heated so as to preserve his possessions from damp, but the cellar there was not large enough to accommodate all the fuel he needed. Besides, some of the furniture was stored in the cellar at Whyniard's. It was so lucky, John Johnson said, that Master Percy had been able to hire this fine vaulted cellar that nobody wanted, so that he could lay in supplies for next winter.

The conspirators carefully arranged the wooden billets on top of the stones and iron bars that hid the barrels of gunpowder. They did this work with great thoroughness so that not an inch of anything but wood was to be seen. Now everything was ready for the Opening of Parliament on October 3rd.

But it was only April. They had to keep the secret, and also keep themselves for six months. Robert Catesby, always the leader, called a meeting of the conspirators in the ground-floor room of Whyniard's house.

"In getting possession of the vault under Parliament House," he said, "we have had a stroke of good fortune such as none of us dreamed of. All our preparations are made there. Now it is better that none of us should go near the vault, not even John Johnson," he smiled at Guy Fawkes, "even that valuable and trusted servant, should only go occasionally in the coming months to make sure that all is well.

"But we are in a difficult situation. The first of our difficulties is money. We have spent what we had on gunpowder and wood. I have been paying the rent of my house across the river, and the rent of this house, and the hire of the vault. I am cleaned out, gentlemen, I know that most of us are in the same case. What are we to do?"

There was a thoughtful silence; since they were all known to be Catholic none of them could get employment. Tom Percy was lucky because he lived in the household of his cousin, who supported him in return for his services, and, as the custom was, kept him supplied with horses, servants and clothes, but did not pay him a salary. Robert Winter, who, for some months, had been supplying the conspirators with money to live on, did not

42

dare to draw any more from his estate for fear it should be noticed.

"We must scatter for the time being," Robert Catesby said. "Each must look after himself as best he can. But we must have money for our plans. We need arms and horses for the uprising in the Midlands. I can see only one way of getting funds; we must add to our number. We must carefully select and invite to join us one or two loyal and devout Catholics who are also rich."

"Have you such in mind?" Jack Wright asked.

"I can think of several," Catesby said. "But here I want to ask something of you all. I believe that I know one or two men who might join us, and who would be willing and able to supply money for the cause; they are men known to you too, Tom Percy. But I think that since they have rich estates and also young children they might only consent to join us if they could do so in secret. If their names are known to me and to Tom Percy, would you be willing, the rest of you, not to know who they are, if I find that they will only give their support on those terms?"

There was a silence. The conspirators looked moody and doubtful. They did not like it much. To have others admitted to this secret but not know who those others were? It was asking a lot of them. They had been willing to take the full risk. Why should these newcomers not do the same? Why could not Catesby tell them the names of these people? They were all in danger and the danger ought to be equally shared.

"What do you say, Guy?" Catesby asked.

"That I do not like it. That you should try to find men who are willing to take the same risk as we do, and to let their names be known to us since they are bound to know ours."

"And if I cannot find such men?"

"Then I suppose you must do as you suggest. But unless

you can answer for these men as for yourself, it would be better to manage without their money."

Catesby looked round the uneasy group. He exerted all his charm, all his power of commanding and persuading other men.

"What I am asking all of you to do is to trust me." He jerked forward the hilt of his sword and laid his hand on the engraving of the crucifixion. "I swear by Christ's death that I will ask no man to join us unless I can answer for him as for myself. Are you satisfied?"

"We must be," Guy Fawkes said. "If you cannot find men who are prepared to trust the rest of us, and to put their lives in our hands as ours will be in theirs."

He guessed that Robin Catesby, who was inclined to act first and to ask his fellow conspirators to agree afterwards, had already approached the men he was thinking of, and that they must have demanded that their names should only be known to Catesby and to Percy.

The other young men, who were all devoted to Robin Catesby and admired him with an enthusiasm that Guy Fawkes did not entirely share, were more easily satisfied.

"We will trust you, Robin. Choose men for whom you can answer as for yourself, and we need ask no further."

"Let them give us their money," Jack Wright said, "and they are truly committed to our cause. They can keep their names to themselves."

Catesby turned to Guy Fawkes.

"For you, Guy, I have a plan. For the moment, there is nothing more for John Johnson to do. His master Tom Percy can send him into the country on some errand and himself keep the keys of this house and of the vault. As soon as we can raise some money, Guy, my plan is that you should sail again to the Low Countries, and should see our good Catholic friends who are soldiering there, Sir

William Stanley and Captain Hugh Owen. You should tell them of our plan. They are brave and experienced soldiers; as soon as the uprising starts in this country they are the men whom we shall need to command our levies. Are you willing, all of you, that Guy should reveal our plan to Stanley and Owen?"

"So long as they take the oath," Robert Keyes said. "They must be told nothing; nothing at all until they have heard Mass with Guy and have received the Sacrament with him, and sworn on the Missal not to reveal what he tells them to anyone else in the world."

"I will see that they do that," Guy Fawkes said grimly. "They shall know nothing until after they have taken the oath." He thought that too many people were now being admitted to the secret.

"I shall not broach the matter with them at all, unless I think them suitable," he added.

Catesby, who knew that he could manage all the others together more easily than he could manage Guy Fawkes, made haste to agree.

"By May, Guy, you shall have funds for your journey. The rest of you must scatter for a time, but keep me informed as to where you are. I will at once approach the men I am thinking of and ask them for funds for our cause. Then I will prepare for the uprising in the Midlands, and I shall need some of you to help me. I have already found a place to store arms near Ashby St. Leger. And I have a horse breeder, a good Catholic, Master Benock, who knows every stable in the district. He is making a list for me of the strongest and swiftest horses in Catholic hands."

The plotters separated, glad to get out of their cramped quarters in Whyniard's house, but uneasy about the long wait of six months during which the secret must be kept. Catesby went off with Tom Percy to Bath where the Earl of Northumberland had some lodgings which he was quite willing to lend to his cousin. Guy Fawkes prepared for the journey to the Netherlands. The other young men went to the homes of their families or friends to wait for a summons from Catesby or, if none came, until October 3rd.

Chapter 7
A Time of Waiting

In Bath, Robert Catesby and Tom Percy settled down for some weeks in the comfortable lodgings lent to them by the Earl of Northumberland.

It was a great relief not to have to spend the daylight hours chipping at a hard stone wall, and to be able to go to bed at night instead of carrying heavy sacks of chippings outside and digging holes for them in the garden.

Catesby revealed to Tom Percy the names of the men he wanted to ask to join the conspiracy and to contribute money for it.

"We need zealous Catholics, thoroughly trustworthy, but still rich enough to be able to help us with funds. So many Catholics have been heavily fined, and have lost their estates, that it limits the number of men we can choose from. I have three in mind—Ambrose Rookwood, Everard Digby and Francis Tresham."

They discussed the three men, all of whom Tom Percy also knew. He agreed that they would be suitable, and was quite willing that Robin should approach them.

Robin Catesby rode first to visit Ambrose Rookwood at his home, Coldham Hall near Bury St. Edmunds in Suffolk.

Rookwood was the head of an old Catholic family, who had refused to abandon their religion during the reign of Queen Elizabeth I. They had been punished for their obstinacy; Ambrose Rookwood had just appeared before a Court of Sessions, and had been declared a recusant because he refused to attend the services of the Church of England.

There was a secret chapel in Coldham Hall, which was so arranged that it looked like an ordinary room, except when Mass was being said there. Close to it was a hiding hole for priests, with an entrance behind one of the panels in the hall. Ambrose Rookwood had lived undisturbed with his charming wife and his two boys. He had given shelter to a good many priests and had heard them say Mass, so far without interruption. But he often wondered how long this luck was likely to last since the King had declared his intention of dealing even more strictly with Catholics.

Ambrose Rookwood was not only devoted to his religion. Like most of the other people who knew him, he was devoted to Robin Catesby. There would have been no gunpowder plot at all but for Catesby's strong influence over his friends. Ambrose Rookwood was so eager to imitate Robin in every way that he too had the crucifixion engraved on his sword.

When he learned that there was a secret enterprise to defend the Catholic faith, in which Robin wanted him to share, he immediately took the oath of secrecy.

The two young men heard Mass together in Rookwood's private chapel and Catesby told him about the gunpowder plot. Rookwood agreed to join, although he well knew that he risked his estate and his life, and the happiness of his wife and children. He was quite willing to contribute money; better spend it that way than pay it in fines as he might be ordered to do at any moment. Catesby rode back to Bath through the leafy summer lanes very well content with his new recruit.

On June 9th of that year, 1605, King James summoned all the judges in the country to a conference. He spoke to them himself, urging them to ferret out all the notable Catholics in their district and to enforce the full penalties of the law on them. Cecil, the most bitter enemy of the Catholics, was made Earl of Salisbury, as a reward for his services.

Guy Fawkes came back from the Low Countries without much to report. Sir William Stanley had gone off to Spain. Captain Owen, to whom Guy Fawkes revealed the secret, did not think it likely that Stanley, who was hoping to receive a pardon from King James, would take any part in the conspiracy. Captain Owen was not eager to come back to England himself. He was fully engaged in fighting for Spain in the Netherlands.

There was other discouraging news for the plotters. During this summer another child, Princess Mary, was born to the King and Queen. This meant that the conspirators would have to seize her as well as Princess Elizabeth and Prince Charles. They would not be able to risk leaving one of the King's children free, perhaps to be brought up as a Protestant and some day to claim the throne.

Guy Fawkes went back to Whyniard's house, and took up his role again as John Johnson. Tom Percy came back to the Earl of Northumberland's London house. They had some money now, provided by Ambrose Rookwood. They bought more barrels of gunpowder, being careful to buy them here and there, a few at a time. They stored them all by night in the vault under Parliament House, and covered them with the logs of wood.

At the end of July, a Royal Proclamation was issued to announce that the Opening of Parliament had been postponed from October 7th to November 5th. This further change of date shook the nerves of the conspirators. Why was the Opening always postponed? Had the King any idea, however vague, that the opening of the next Parliament might be a dangerous occasion for him? Tom Percy was asked to find out through his cousin, but he could not hear of anything to suggest that the King was uneasy about the Opening of Parliament.

James I was never in a hurry to see Parliament again, he preferred ruling without them. But he had probably made this postponement because it fitted in better with his plans for the hunting season.

Robert Catesby rode to see Sir Everard Digby, who lived at Gothurst in Buckinghamshire. Everard Digby was young, handsome, dashing, married to a beautiful and very rich wife, the father of promising young children.

Digby was one of the richest landowners in the Midlands. His house contained the most cunningly concealed priest's hiding hole in the country. A secret passage from the hall led to a small room with floorboards which could be moved easily, that covered pivots. An opening in the floor could be made immediately, and any threatened priest could drop down into a cubbyhole below, pulling the floorboards into place behind him.

Digby was devoted to Robert Catesby, who trusted him so completely that he did not even ask him to swear the usual oath. When they were out riding together, Catesby held out his dagger to Digby so that he grasped the cross-shaped hilt.

"Take this cross in your hand, Everard, and swear never to reveal what I shall now tell you."

Digby swore but when Catesby told him about the gunpowder plot, he was horrified.

"I will have no part in it!" he exclaimed. "I will take no part in such a violent deed!"

"I do not ask you to take part in it," Catesby retorted.

"You will not be there. You will see nothing of it. All I ask you to do is to arrange a hunting party near Combe Abbey and to invite your Catholic friends to it. Then, when you get the word, you will ride to Combe Abbey, seize the Princess Elizabeth and hold her in safe keeping. You will take her easily enough if you collect a strong party. There will be no bloodshed. To protect a child during the disturbances that will follow the sudden destruction of King and Parliament, that is all I am asking you to do; that and to help us with some money for we are all poor men, and have already spent what we have."

At first, Digby would not hear of taking any part in the conspiracy nor of contributing a penny to it. He could not bear the idea of helping to send so many warm, vigorous, living people to a sudden death. However like the other young men he could not stand firm against Catesby. He resisted for a few days but, before he fully realized what had happened, he was as deeply involved in the plot as any of them. He undertook to seize Princess Elizabeth when the day came; and he handed over fifteen hundred crowns.

It was he who suggested to Catesby that gunpowder which had been stored for so many months, first in the cellar of Whyniard's house, then in the vault below Parliament House, might be getting damp. Guy Fawkes was instructed to look at it and found that some of the barrels that they had bought first were damp. He and Tom Winter disposed of them and bought fresh supplies with Digby's money. They took the new barrels by night into the vault, and covered them with wooden blocks.

Meanwhile, Robert Catesby was enrolling the last of the conspirators, Francis Tresham.

Tresham, who was thirty seven years old, was Catesby's first cousin. He came of a devoted Catholic family who had been fined for refusing to give up their faith. Francis

Tresham himself had taken part in a rebellion against Queen Elizabeth I. He was reckless, hot-tempered and impulsive. Catesby found him much easier to persuade than Everard Digby had been. Tresham was ripe for mischief. He contributed money and promised to take part in the uprising.

There were now thirteen conspirators. And as it happened, by chance, it was the thirteenth man, the last one to join, who ruined them.

It was arranged that some days before the 5th of November, Guy Fawkes should lay the mine in position in the cellar. It was he who was to fire the fuse that would set off the mine. He was to use a slow match that should give him a quarter of an hour before the explosion during which to make his own escape.

As soon as Parliament House blew up, Catesby, who would be in London, would ride to the Midlands to take command of the uprising. Tom Percy, who being often at court, knew his way about the Palace of Whitehall, would seize the young Prince Charles. Digby would assemble his supposed hunting party, and ride to Combe Abbey and take Princess Elizabeth. Some of the conspirators would seize the baby Princess Mary. All the Catholic gentry who had been warned to expect an uprising would ride to London where they would proclaim Princess Elizabeth Queen.

The plan was complete by the last week in October. Guy Fawkes, still playing the part of that sober and almost unnoticeable servant John Johnson, went quietly to and fro between Whyniard's house and the vault below Parliament House. Everybody in the area was used to seeing him about in his servent's livery, with his expressionless face which never seemed to show any kind of feeling. No one could have guessed that in a few days' time he expected to play the central part in a wholesale murder at great risk to his own life.

Chapter 8
The Thirteenth Conspirator

As the time drew near, Robert Catesby and Tom Winter made their headquarters in a house called White Webbs, which was near Barnet, on the outskirts of London. It was not too far for Guy Fawkes to ride out and join them sometimes, when there was anything they wanted to discuss with him. White Webbs had another advantage. It was equipped with several hiding holes and secret passages. If by any chance anybody should become suspicious and should come to look for Catesby and Winter, they could hide themselves in a few minutes.

One morning in the last week of October, they were sitting in the hall of White Webbs with Guy Fawkes, who had arrived late in the evening of the previous day. The three of them were putting the finishing touches to their plans.

Suddenly, they heard the sound of a horseman galloping up the avenue. Everyone moved quickly to the window. Their nerves were on edge; they were afraid that this might be a messenger with bad news, somebody come to warn them that the vault had been searched or the Opening of Parliament was postponed again.

The approaching rider was a fair-haired young man with a rich fur-lined cloak falling back from a doublet of slashed cloth and velvet. His horse was lathered with sweat

although it was a cold morning. He dismounted at the door, flung the reins to a servant, and ran into the house.

"It is only Francis Tresham," Catesby said, in tones of relief.

Guy Fawkes stroked his beard but made no answer. He would never have invited Francis Tresham to join them. He thought him a very unstable man, rash and careless in his talk.

Tresham was pale and his eyes looked wild. "Robin," he said to Catesby, "I must speak to you privately."

"You can safely speak before Tom Winter and Guy Fawkes. Everything that I know is known to them."

"No, I must speak to you alone. This is a family matter."

"You will excuse us." Catesby led Francis Tresham into another room. "Now tell me what is troubling you, Frank."

"Robin," Tresham said earnestly. "This must not be."

"What do you mean?"

"This gunpowder plot. We cannot blow up Parliament House on the day of opening. Both my brothers-in-law will be there. My sisters—I cannot do this to them. I should have thought of it before."

Catesby regretted that Tresham had thought of it now. He realized that this needed very careful handling if it was not to ruin the whole plan.

"Sit down, Frank. Calm yourself. Tell me what is in your mind."

"You know that one of my sisters is married to Lord Mounteagle, the other to Lord Stanton. Both lords will be at the Opening of Parliament on November 5th. And I myself love Mounteagle as a brother. I cannot go on with this. We must abandon the plot."

"You are bound to the plot by your oath, Francis."

"I did wrong to swear such an oath."

"But you did swear it. We have all sworn it. You are bound to us and to the enterprise. And everything is ready. For the sake of all the Catholics in this country who suffer constant persecution, we must go through with it now."

"Then at least I must warn Mounteagle."

Catesby thought that it would be impossible to devise any kind of warning that would not betray their secret. But he saw that Tresham was in a dangerous state of excitement. He had always been reckless; in his present mood he might do anything; he might even break the oath to save his sisters' husbands.

"I understand your feeling," Catesby said slowly, "perhaps we can find a way."

"I can only think of one way to save both of them Robin, let us give up the plot. I do not like it. I do not want to destroy so many people. Why, the Lords are nearly all known to us or to our friends. Let us abandon it, and think of another way."

"How can we abandon our purpose with the vault below Parliament House stocked with barrels of gunpowder? How could we move them when the time of the Opening is so near? You must be mad, Frank."

"I think it is you who are mad, Robin. Fool that I was not to see it before."

Catesby was thinking quickly. Tresham was no longer to be trusted, that was clear. Would it be better to call in Guy Fawkes and Tom Winter? The three of them could overpower Tresham, and shut him up in the priest's hiding hole until after November 5th. But suppose Tresham had told friends that he was riding out to White Webbs and they came to look for him when he did not return? And was the priest's hiding hole strong enough to hold him? Not unless one of them stayed behind to keep guard, which, as they planned to leave the house before November 5th, they could not do. Catesby wished that he had never told Frank Tresham anything about the plot. True he had contributed money but it looked as if they might pay dearly for the loan.

"I wish I had never heard of your gunpowder plot," Tresham cried. He added, "You asked me the other day for more money. I will give you none, no more till after November 5th."

Catesby determined to use all his powers of persuasion.

Had he not enlisted the whole group by the charm of his own personality? He did not think that it would fail him now. He put a hand on Tresham's arm.

"Frank, hear me a minute. You are bound by your oath as we all are. It is too late to draw back. You are too good a friend and companion to leave me now. I understand your concern for your brothers-in-law, but many men have died for the Catholic faith and, if we do not take violent action, many more will suffer. You would be ready yourself to die for your religion?"

"Most certainly."

"Then you must be ready, if necessary, to kill for it."

"But not my sisters' husbands. I cannot do that to my dear Mounteagle."

"I will talk about this to Winter and Fawkes, and between us we will devise some way of preventing Mounteagle and Stanton from going to the House for the Opening. But it must be done at the last minute." Catesby laid his hand again on Tresham's arm, and smiled into his sullen face.

"I have always loved you, Frank. Do you not trust me?"

"I trust you in most things, Robin," Tresham said rather doubtfully. "And I love you too. But I must be sure that Mounteagle and Stanton are safe."

"So you shall be. I am going back to London tomorrow. Come to me at my lodging, Frank, on the day before the Opening, November 4th, and I will tell you what plan I have been able to make to warn the two lords. Will that content you?"

Tresham nodded but he did not look entirely satisfied.

"You will swear to me, Frank, that you will speak of this to no one? As you love me, you will keep our secret till the day?"

"I am not a traitor," Tresham said stiffly.

"I know you are not. I know you are true."

Tresham, refusing to stay for wine or food, ran out of the house, mounted his horse and rode off. Catesby went back to Guy Fawkes and Tom Winter, and told them what had happened.

Guy Fawkes was dismayed. He thought that it would have been much safer to clap Tresham into the priest's hiding hole and keep him there till after November 5th, but it was too late to do that now. He said emphatically, "There must be no question of giving any kind of warning to Mounteagle or Stanton. When Tresham comes to your lodging on November 4th, he must be put out of the way if you are not sure of him. He must be knocked on the head and carried by night to your house in the Lambeth marshes, and locked in the cellar and left there until after the explosion. His brothers-in-law must share the same fate as all the enemies of our religion."

Chapter 9
The Unsigned Letter

Lord Mounteagle, a handsome, lively young man in his early thirties, had been a great friend of Robert Catesby's and had taken part with him in the Essex revolt against Queen Elizabeth. He had been a Catholic, but lately he had written to the King to tell him that he had been converted to the Protestant religion; perhaps his conversion was real, but he was probably influenced by the knowledge that so few opportunities were open to Catholics.

Mounteagle's conversion had naturally made a coolness between him and Catesby, who was also far too preoccupied with the gunpowder plot to have time for anyone whose sympathies would be against it. Lord Mounteagle, who had married Elizabeth Tresham, lived at Hoxton in a house which she had lately inherited from her father. Hoxton, though only four miles from London, was in those days a country village surrounded by green fields.

On the evening of October 26th, Mounteagle, who had been staying with friends in the country for the hunting, arrived back at his own home. He sent one of his servants out on an errand to the village, and sat down to his supper.

While he was being served with the first dishes, the servant came back bringing a sealed letter.

"This was given me, my Lord, by a man who came up to me in the street. He asked me to put it into your hand without delay."

Lord Mounteagle glanced at the letter. "A man who came up to you in the street! What was he like?"

"I could not see in the dark, my Lord, except that he was a reasonably tall man. He must have seen me in the light from a doorway and recognized your livery."

Mounteagle opened the letter and saw a cramped, unfamiliar handwriting. He was tired and hungry after a day's hunting and a long ride. He tossed the letter to a young gentleman of his household, Thomas Warde, who was sitting at table with him.

"A begging letter by the look of it. Read it aloud to me,"

Warde slowly read:

> My Lord. Out of the love I bear to some of your friends I have a care of your preservation, therefore I would advise you as you tender your life to devise some excuse to shift your attendance at this Parliament, for God and man hath concurred to punish the wickedness of this time, and think not slightly of this advertisement but retire yourself into your country where you may expect the event in safety, for though there be no appearance of any stir yet I say they shall receive a terrible blow this Parliament, and yet they shall not see who hurts them. This counsel is not to be contemned, because it may do you good and can do you no harm, for the danger is passed as soon as you have burnt the letter, and I hope God will give you the grace to make good use of it, to whose holy protection I commend you.

Thomas Warde stopped reading.

Lord Mounteagle frowned. "Well? Who has written this letter?"

"My Lord, it is not signed."

"Let me see it."

Mounteagle read the letter through again. "Odds my life!" he muttered. "Who can this man be? Someone who supposes himself to be my friend, and warns me not to attend the Opening of Parliament if I value my life? 'I say they shall receive a terrible blow this Parliament, and yet shall not see who hurts them.' The danger, whatever it may be, will pass as quickly as a letter can be burnt. Is this some madman, or is there a real danger threatening the Opening of Parliament? How do you interpret it, Tom?"

"Perhaps, my Lord, some jest?"

"I do not think so. At least I am very sure that I will try to find out."

"How will you do that, my Lord, when you do not know the name of the writer?"

"I will place the letter in the hands of those whose business it is to find out, and who have the power and the means to do it."

Lord Mounteagle drank his glass of wine and pushed his chair back.

"Order them to saddle Blackbird, Tom, and tell one of the grooms to attend me."

"Is it necessary to ride tonight, my Lord? It is so late and dark, you have had a long day in the saddle, and you have hardly eaten."

"I think there may be no time to lose." Lord Mounteagle turned as he was leaving the room.

"Tom. Not a word of this letter to anybody. Not a whisper. It must be for you as though you had not read it. Do not forget."

Lord Mounteagle mounted his horse, and rode so fast over the muddy, unlit lanes that his groom had hard work to keep up with him.

Windows were still brightly lit in the new Palace of Whitehall, and torches were burning at the gates of the courtyard. Mounteagle had friends at court and was well-known to everybody in the Palace. When they recognized him the sentries admitted him. He dismounted, threw his reins to his groom, strode across the Great Court, and climbed the stairs to the Royal Rooms.

To the Captain of the Beefeaters in the guard room he said, "Mounteagle. I would have audience of the King *now* on urgent business which concerns his safety."

The Captain let him go through to the inner door, but there one of the Gentlemen of the Household told him that the King was away.

"His Majesty has been hunting all day in Hertfordshire, and has sent a messenger to say that he will sleep in his hunting lodge at Royston so that the hunt may make an early start tomorrow morning."

"Is the Earl of Salisbury here?"

"Yes, my Lord. The Earl of Suffolk dines with him, and the Lord Chamberlain."

"I must see them."

After some delay, Mounteagle was ushered into a room warmed by a big fire, and bright with candlelight. The company round the table had finished their dishes of meat and their salads. They were picking at the sweetmeats in the small gold dishes and drinking their wine. Mounteagle saw that the Lord Chamberlain sat on Salisbury's right, the Earl of Suffolk on his left. Opposite to him was Charles Howard, the Lord High Admiral of England. He saw, too, the Earl of Northampton and the Earl of Worcester, two men high in the esteem of the King.

Mounteagle was very glad that he had come. He was ambitious and these were all men whose approval it would be well worth his while to win. As a Catholic who had only lately become a Protestant, he knew that he might still be partly suspect to them. Whether the letter was worth taking seriously or not—he thought it was—he wanted to show himself in this high company as being alert to the least hint of danger to the King and Parliament.

"I beg your pardon, my Lords, for disturbing you in this unmannerly way," he said. "But I received this letter an hour ago. It was handed to one of my servants by a stranger in the dark. When I read it I did not know if it was the work of a madman, or whether it was by the hand of someone who knew of a real danger threatening the safety of the King and the Lords and Commons. I am happy to commit it to you, my Lord of Salisbury, for your judgement."

Cecil spread out the letter on the table and moved one of the heavy gold candlesticks nearer to throw more light on it. He made a beckoning motion with his hand to the Lord Chamberlain who came round to read over his shoulder. There was silence while the two were reading. When they had finished, they looked at each other with meaning.

Cecil passed the letter to the Lord High Admiral. He said thoughtfully, "Reports have come to me lately from my people on the Continent that it was known in the Low Countries that Catholics in England were planning some kind of a disturbance to mark the Opening of Parliament on November 5th."

He turned to Mounteagle. "You know nothing at all about this letter? You can make no guess at the writer?"

"No, my Lord."

"You did right to bring it to me. I shall show it to His Majesty."

"My only care, my Lord, was for the safety of the King and State."

Cecil made no answer to that. He disliked and distrusted Catholics so much that he could not bring himself to be very encouraging to a man who had been a Catholic until lately. Mounteagle might have been honestly converted to the Church of England or he might have changed his religion for safety and advancement. On the whole, the Earl of Salisbury preferred those Catholics who were loyal to their faith and could, therefore, be soundly punished. He was not going to be over-grateful to Lord Mounteagle, nor was he going to admit him to their counsels.

"I am sorry," he said, "that you have another ride

before you when it is so late and dark. You are accompanied by some of your household, I hope?"

"A groom, my Lord. I did not stay for the others."

"Then we must not keep you."

Mounteagle saluted the illustrious company and left the room.

The Earl of Salisbury tapped the letter with his skinny fingers. "Gentlemen, I do believe that we may have here a clue to a dangerous conspiracy. We can do nothing at the moment but watch and wait. Let none of us speak of it outside this room. Tomorrow evening when he returns from hunting I shall show it to the King."

Chapter 10
A Warning

Thomas Warde, the young man in the household of Lord Mounteagle who had read the unsigned letter aloud, happened to be a friend of Thomas Winter. On the next day, October 28th, he went into London to see Winter at his lodgings. Warde had been thinking about the letter. At first, it had seemed to him that it must be a joke. Then he saw that Lord Mounteagle took it very seriously. He began to wonder if it conveyed news of a Catholic Plot.

It might be a real plot or it might be an imaginary plot trumped up by enemies to discredit Catholics and to justify further persecutions. Such things had happened. Whichever it was, it was not unlikely that Tom Winter might be involved in it. Tom Warde thought he would like to find out if Winter knew anything. If he did not it might be as well to drop a hint that something was brewing. Perhaps, Tom Warde thought, he could do this without exactly telling Winter about the letter, since Lord Mounteagle had ordered him to keep it secret.

What happened was that he told Tom Winter all about the letter, because he enjoyed telling such a dramatic story.

"And my Lord put down his knife and fork and drained a glass of wine at a gulp, and shouted for a fresh horse. And although he was weary from a day's hunting, he rode

off to Whitehall with the letter. I do not know what he did there; when I asked him he said that the King was away hunting, but he had seen some of his Councillors. He was very short-tempered all this morning. There is something in the wind, and I thought you should know of it."

"Thanks," Tom Winter said, after a short pause. He looked dismayed, but was clearly not going to say anything more. Thomas Warde left him and rode back to Hoxton.

Very early next day, Tom Winter called for his horse and rode out to White Webbs, where Catesby and Fawkes were together.

Tom Winter told his story. "So we are betrayed," he concluded. "But who can have written the letter?"

Catesby, who had immediately thought "Tresham" did not answer. He believed it would be better to deal with

Francis Tresham himself. He did not want the other young men to make themselves conspicuous at this moment by fighting Tresham.

"We must give up the plot now," Tom Winter cried. "We must fly overseas. There is nothing left for us but to get out of England. I shall offer my sword to the Spanish army in the Netherlands."

"You go too fast, Tom," Catesby said. "This letter tells nothing of our plot. It is only a shot in the dark. It does not mention a single name. It does not speak of gunpowder nor of the vault. There is nothing to lead Cecil's spies to us."

"They will learn from this that something sudden is intended for the day of the Opening of Parliament. Anyone who was not a complete fool — and Salisbury is not that — would examine the Parliament House and all its surroundings at once. Probably by now they have searched the vault and Whyniard's house."

"If so, they may have seen nothing but a large stock of fuel for Master Percy's use. But we can find out if they have searched. Here is John Johnson the caretaker, who has the keys of Whyniard's and of the vault. He will ride back to London with you and will look round the house and the vault and make sure that all is well."

"If the King and Salisbury have guessed the truth and found the gunpowder, they will have posted soldiers in the vault. You are asking Guy to ride straight into a trap."

"If I had been playing the part of John Johnson," Catesby said, "I would ride in myself. I ask no man to do what I would not dare to do. Are you willing, Guy?"

Guy Fawkes nodded. Of course he would go, it was a necessary part of what he had undertaken.

"I will ride alone," he said to Catesby. "Tom had better stay here with you. We do not want to show any more of

69

ourselves than we need in Westminster."

Guy Fawkes rode into London at a steady pace. He dismounted at the door of Whyniard's house, tethered his horse to the iron ring by the door, unlocked the door and stepped inside with the ordinary manner of a caretaker entering a house that he was looking after.

The house was empty and everything was just as he had left it. The conspirators had rolled a chest up against the place in the cellar where they had, with so much difficulty, made a hole in the wall. The chest was covered with dust, so it had not been moved. During the summer and autumn, grass and weeds had grown over the top of the pits where they had buried the rubble in the garden.

Guy Fawkes went out of Whyniard's house and round to the Parliament House. He would not have been human if he had not felt a shiver of fear. Here was the real clue to their secret. Here, if anything had been discovered, soldiers would be waiting for him. He had lately oiled the big key. He fitted it into the lock and opened the door.

It would be obvious at once if any searcher had discovered the hidden gunpowder, since he had arranged the logs of wood over it in a certain pattern.

He walked boldly across the cellar towards the piles of fuel, which he could only just see in the dim light from two gratings high up in the wall. He showed no sign of nervousness or hesitation. He was John Johnson, doing his proper duty by inspecting his master's stock of firewood. But Guy knew very well that if the cellar had been searched, if there were soldiers standing back in the darkness, he had no chance of escape.

His footsteps rang on the stone floor. He heard their echo from the far end of the vault. He waited for a spring or a shot. Nobody moved, nothing stirred. Guy Fawkes came up to the stack of firewood.

Even in the dim light he knew that it had not been touched. The logs were arranged in just the same pattern as he had left them. Nobody had disturbed them.

The cellar was empty; no soldiers were lying in wait for him. This meant that so far neither Salisbury nor anybody else had guessed that whatever danger the unsigned letter referred to might come from the vault below Parliament House. John Johnson carefully arranged the billets in a slightly different pattern, then went out and locked the door again.

He rode back to White Webbs to tell Robin Catesby and Tom Winter that so far all was well.

Chapter 11
The King's Command

On October 31st, King James arrived back at his Palace of Whitehall. He had enjoyed a good day's hunting, and only returned in the evening just in time for dinner, which was always served to him with great ceremony. The King, who had been poor as King of Scotland, still kept some notions of economy. He had cut down the number of meat dishes at one meal from thirty to twenty four, but he liked these dishes to be served to him by noblemen who knelt to offer them to him. These noblemen were always richly dressed in velvet and satin, but the King himself preferred to dress plainly, often no more finely than any simple country gentleman. He frequently wore a plain grey suit, and a long black cloak lined with crimson. Only in his jewels he had no taste for austerity. He liked to wear a necklace of diamonds below his plain starched ruff, and he generally had a magnificent diamond or some other jewel in his hatband.

On this evening of October 31st, James talked to the courtiers round him about the hunt, which was his passion. Lord Salisbury was far too experienced to try and discuss the business of the nation, until the King had followed every deer to the kill. Cecil knew how to wait; but he also knew that he could not afford to wait too long before showing the letter Mounteagle had brought to the King.

There were only five days before the Opening of Parliament.

On the next day, November 1st, Lord Salisbury came as early as he dared to the Private Gallery where the King did most of his business. It was a long gallery, beautifully decorated. Here the King generally received ambassadors, or other visitors from foreign countries; here he assembled his Council. This morning he was alone with his chief Minister. The small, pale, hunchbacked Cecil, dressed as always in black though his doublet was of rich material, carried a pile of state papers which had been waiting for the King's attention. On top of the pile was the unsigned letter addressed to Lord Mounteagle.

"There is something here which I think Your Majesty should see at once."

"Well, what is it?" the King asked in a peevish tone. It always took him a day to settle down to his royal business after a good hunt.

"It is an unsigned letter addressed to Lord Mounteagle. It was handed to one of his servants in the village of Hoxton, after dark, by an unknown man who immediately slipped away. Mounteagle brought it to me at once the night before last . . . as he was right to do," Cecil added grudgingly. It was not so much that he wanted to do justice to Mounteagle as that he wanted to impress the importance of the letter on the King, who in his present mood might, Cecil thought, toss it aside.

James slowly read the letter. Having finished, he grunted, turned the paper over, examined the broken seal, then read the letter through again.

Salisbury waited in silence. He had made up his own mind that the letter indicated a Catholic plot to set fire to the Parliament House at the Opening or to blow it up. After working with the King for two years, he understood his

master. James liked to be the one who *knew,* the one who pointed out to his ministers how things stood and what to do about them. It would all go more easily if he could tell Salisbury what the letter meant, much better than if Salisbury had to tell him. And the King was no fool, he had a scholar's mind, he was quick to see the meaning of any written word. Salisbury waited with real interest for his master's opinion.

James frowned at the letter and handed it back. In the broad Scotch accent which he had not lost in two years on the throne of England he said, "This is no joke."

"I am of your opinion, Sire."

"It is a serious matter to be considered seriously. Listen to this, my Lord. *They shall receive a terrible blow this Parliament, and yet shall not see who hurts them.* The meaning of that is plain," the King said. "Do you understand it?"

Salisbury, who thought he did, looked doubtful.

"Why, man, use your wits. It's plain enough. They mean to blow us all up with gunpowder."

"I believe you may be right, Sire."

"It would not be the first time such a thing has been perpetrated against my family. Mr father, Lord Darnley, was, you will remember, blown up with gunpowder by the Scottish Lords."

"I remember well, Sire."

"This then is the meaning of the letter. You see the writer says, *the danger is passed as soon as you have burnt the letter,* which is the same as to say that the danger is as swift as the burning of a piece of paper. Indeed, my Lord, we have been very near to destruction. Let us be thankful that our good Mounteagle brought the letter to you."

Cecil nodded. He did not like Mounteagle but he never

75

contradicted the King except on a matter of great importance.

James said thoughtfully, "There must be cellars or vaults of some kind underneath the Parliament House. Otherwise these people, whoever they are, could not hide enough gunpowder, and lay a mine. Will you find out and have the whole place most thoroughly searched before the Opening?"

"I will, Sire."

The next day, the Earl of Salisbury came again to the King in the Private Gallery. He brought with him the Lord Chamberlain.

"We have come to consult with you, Sire, as to when the cellars under the Parliament House should be searched. We have to think first of preserving Your Majesty and the Houses of Parliament on this occasion. But we shall best serve that purpose by finding out who the men are who have dared to plan this wickedness. It is important to take them in the act so that they cannot do any further harm. I think, Sire, and the Lord Chamberlain agrees with me, that we should not make a full search of Parliament House before the evening of November 4th. If there is a plot to use gunpowder, all preparations must be finished by then, and it is likely that the plotters will be in their places ready for action, or if not they will be near and we can set a watch and seize them when they come. Do you agree, Sire?"

"It is leaving it very late to take action," the King said nervously, "but," he added, "I believe you are right. It is of no use to discover the weapon without finding the men who planned to use it. Order a thorough search of the whole building of the Parliament House for the evening of November 4th, and see that I am informed at once if anything dangerous is found there."

Chapter 12
A Second Warning

The conspirators knew more about what was going on than the King or Lord Salisbury supposed.

Somebody at Whitehall talked about the letter. It would certainly not have been Salisbury; probably the King told the Queen and she told her ladies, and one of them could not resist passing on the story. In a very short time there was gossip throughout the court; there were terrible dangers threatening; there was a Catholic Plot; Lord Mounteagle had received an unsigned letter warning him not to attend the Opening of Parliament; he had handed the letter to the Earl of Salisbury, who had shown it to the King.

Francis Tresham, who had friends at court, heard of this talk. In a way he heard it with relief; it showed that his brother-in-law Mounteagle had taken his warning seriously and probably since the King and Cecil were alerted they would act in time to prevent the slaughter of Parliament. Tresham, now that he had time to think this over, away from the stimulating company of Robin Catesby, did not really want the plot to succeed. But he loved Catesby and had other friends among the conspirators. He did not want them to be arrested and perhaps tortured before they were led to their execution.

Tresham decided to warn the others without saying that

he had written the unsigned letter. He sent a message to Tom Winter asking him to meet him after dark in the passage behind Lincoln's Inn which was not far from Winter's lodging in the Strand.

It was a cold, wet evening and there was nobody about in the passage. Tresham and Tom Winter, wrapped to the chin in their cloaks, walked up and down talking quietly.

"I have heard bad news from friends at court," Tresham said. "It seems that Mounteagle received an unsigned letter warning him to keep away from the Opening of Parliament because of some 'terrible blow' that Parliament shall receive. They say that Mounteagle took the letter to Salisbury and that the King has seen it."

This was not such a surprise to Tom Winter as Tresham imagined, since he had already heard about the letter from Thomas Warde.

"We must give up the plot, Tom," Tresham urged. "They will guess what we intend to do. They will search the whole of Parliament House, and come upon our gunpowder in the cellars. Out only hope is to leave the country without loss of time."

"Even if they find the gunpowder there will be nothing to connect it with us. Our plot will fail but we shall be in no danger; we need not go to the Continent."

"They will find out somehow. They will ask who owns the cellar and will discover that it is rented by Tom Percy. Even if they do not force him to confess by torture, they will have ways of learning who are his friends."

"Yes, that is true," Winter agreed. He shivered and dug his chin deeper into the wet collar of his cloak. It looked to him as though their plot was already a failure and all of them were in danger.

"You may be right," he said gloomily. "I must see Robin at once."

He went off to find Catesby who had now come into London and was lodging at a tavern in the Strand, called *The Irish Boy*. Tom Winter repeated to Catesby everything that Francis Tresham had told him.

"So there is nothing for it, is there, but to get out of the country while we can."

"It is clear that they know there is a Catholic Plot," Catesby said. "And of course it was our friend Frank Tresham who wrote the unsigned letter to Mounteagle."

Tom Winter swore a furious oath.

"Oh yes, it was Tresham who came to see me at White Webbs, wailing about the danger to his sisters' husbands. Fool that I was not to clap him in the priest's hole there and leave him to rot. But Tom, everything is not yet lost. They know that there is a plot but they do not know what it is. It must be two days since Mounteagle took the letter to Whitehall, but they have not been to search the cellars. Guy has just left me; he came to report that all was well. The wood he covered the gunpowder with has not been touched since he laid it in place."

"They may search tonight."

"If they do, Guy Fawkes will bring us word. But if they do not, why there are only three days before the Opening of Parliament. We have only to risk ourselves for three more days. I for one do not leave London till I have spoken with Tom Percy, who returns tomorrow. If he agrees with you that we should give up our plan of blowing up Parliament House, then I must agree too, though I shall still work for the uprising in the Midlands."

Tom Winter was as always encouraged by Catesby's bold confidence, and would not refuse to accept his decision, but he was still nervous. He guessed that Tom Percy, who was rash enough for anything, would insist on carrying out the whole plan as long as there was any chance.

He was quite right. On the next day, November 3rd, Percy rode into London and joined Catesby at *The Irish Boy* in the Strand.

Catesby told him the story of the unsigned letter which Mounteagle had taken to the King.

"Two days ago," Catesby said, "the tale of it was running all round Whitehall. Now it is all over London. I myself have heard men speaking of it over their ale in this tavern. Do you not think that the risk is too great, Tom? We must give it up."

"They have not searched the vault?"

"No, Fawkes was here half an hour ago. He reports that the fuel had not been touched. He looks every few hours; John Johnson of course can easily go in and out of the vault where his master's fuel is stored. But it is Fawkes—if we go on with it—who will run the greatest risk. He cannot leave the vault on November 5th until he has set a light to the fuse."

"He is not the man to shrink from the risk," Tom Percy said. "He would dare anything for the Catholic faith, as I would myself. And so would you, Robin. What! Give up now when success may be only two days away? I would as soon hang myself."

In Percy's company Robin Catesby forgot the doubts that had been growing in his mind since Tom Winter's visit.

"And so would I," he exclaimed. "I am with you, Tom. Whatever happens I am with you to the end."

Chapter 13
The First Search

During those first days of November, Guy Fawkes, still playing the part of John Johnson, spent most of his time in Whyniard's house alone. Two or three times a day he went round to the vault under Parliament House to make sure that no one had discovered the gunpowder. He went as usual to buy food for himself, and from time to time he reported to Catesby, who was within easy reach at *The Irish Boy*. But, for long hours, Guy Fawkes was alone in the empty house. He was an exceptionally brave man with a deep, narrow devotion to his faith that blocked his mind to a good many other things. He had always been prepared to die in battle and he was prepared now to die, if necessary, but he was set on blowing up Parliament House first. Even he grew nervous as every hour brought the Opening nearer and also brought more stories that the King and his Ministers were afraid of a Catholic Plot.

But still every time Guy visited the vault the logs of wood were as he had left them. Could the King and Salisbury really be so stupid as not to have taken warning from the letter? Did they really propose to open Parliament on the 5th without making a thorough search of the premises? As November 4th dawned and the morning hours passed, it almost seemed to Guy Fawkes that no one was going to look in the vault.

He went there just before noon and rearranged the logs of wood in another complicated pattern, more for the sake of doing something than for any other reason. He returned to Whyniard's house, ate some cold meat and bread, and occupied himself by sweeping out the room. He liked to keep his quarters in good order. It was a wet afternoon, the sky heavy with low hanging cloud. Dusk came early. About four o'clock Guy Fawkes took his horn lantern and went round to the vault. He lit the candle with his tinder box, and shone the light onto the pile of fuel. Not one log of wood had been moved.

Guy Fawkes was just about to leave the vault when he heard footsteps and voices in the great hall overhead. No doubt cleaners were up there, brushing the carpets and shaking the dust out of the cushions. There would be other preparations to make for next day's ceremony; the Lord Chamberlain's people would have to see that every seat was in order. But Guy did not want to be seen leaving the vault, and there was a chance that somebody might come down to it. If they did there was nowhere to hide. He blew out the candle in his lantern, pinching the wick with his fingers so that there should be no smell of tallow.

He waited for half an hour. The footsteps and voices overhead continued. Fawkes shifted his feet and swung his arms to and fro. It was very cold in the vault. Presently he heard no more sounds overhead. He still waited, hoping to hear the clang of the big doors as the cleaners shut them. What he heard instead were footsteps and voices from the staircase leading down to the vault. He stiffened himself against the wall. Several people, led by a servant carrying a lantern, came into the vault through the doors at the far end.

Guy Fawkes knew the Lord Chamberlain, Thomas Howard Earl of Suffolk, by sight. He did not recognize

Lord Mounteagle nor the pale, anxious-looking man who came with him, but he heard the Lord Chamberlain speak to him.

"Master Whyniard, you rent this cellar as well as your house, I believe. For what purpose do you use it?"

"I do not use it at all, my Lord. It is not I who rent it. It is let, as my own house is let, to Master Thomas Percy of the household of my Lord of Northumberland."

"Thomas Percy," the Lord Chamberlain said as though making a note in his mind. "What does he want with it?"

Whyniard, who felt unhappily that he was in disgrace without knowing why, said, "I do not know, my Lord." He looked nervously round the vault, and added, "There is Master Percy's servant, John Johnson, standing over there in the corner. He will be able to tell you more than I can."

The Lord Chamberlain called out sharply, "You there . . . . Johnson, if that is your name. Come forward."

Guy Fawkes came forward, touching his hat.

A fine, tall fellow, the Lord Chamberlain thought, but sullen looking, and what did he want with a dagger and a pistol in his belt? He looked like a man one would not care to meet in a lonely place after dark. "You are the servant of Master Percy?"

"Yes, my Lord."

"You know me?" the Lord Chamberlain said sharply.

"By sight, my Lord, naturally."

The Lord Chamberlain looked round the cellar.

"There is a great quantity of wood stored here. To whom does it belong?"

"To my master. It is his store of fuel for the winter, for the house next door which he has rented from Master Whyniard."

"Why does he need so much wood?"

"It is cheaper, my Lord, to have it all carted here at

84

once, and then there is no fear of running short if the winter is hard and the roads are blocked by snow, so that supplies are delayed coming into London."

"Give me the lantern."

The Lord Chamberlain took the lantern from his servant's hand and held it high, turning it so that the beams of light explored the whole of the vault. He said to his companions, "There is nothing more to see here. Let us go."

They tramped up the staircase and went out, leaving the

doors open behind them. Guy Fawkes breathed a sigh of relief. What fools they were! That they should have been here, standing only a few yards from the store of gunpowder, that they should have noticed the piles of logs and never even poked a stick into it . . . that they should have been satisfied with his answers . . . it seemed too good to be true.

Chapter 14
Growing Suspicion

The Lord Chamberlain and his companions walked away from the Parliament House towards the Palace of Whitehall.

During the short walk the Lord Chamberlain only spoke once; he said half to himself, "Thomas Percy lives in the household of his cousin the Earl of Northumberland, and travels about on his affairs. Why should he need such a large stock of fuel for a house which he hardly ever uses and which is mostly left in the care of a servant?"

Whyniard, puzzled and uneasy, did not know whether to answer or not. He felt that he had somehow been at fault in renting his house to Thomas Percy, but the Earl of Northumberland had asked him personally to cut short Ferris's lease because his cousin needed the house for his service. Now Whyniard felt that the Lord Chamberlain was angry with him for letting it to Percy. It was very difficult to keep on the right track in these troubled times.

Mounteagle, whose chief concern at the moment was to show himself a good Protestant and a loyal servant of King James, said eagerly, "Thomas Percy is a very devout Catholic. In Yorkshire they call him 'the Chief Pillar of the Papacy' and he is a man of a most fiery nature who would dare anything."

The Lord Chamberlain grunted but made no other

reply. At the gateway of the Palace he dismissed Whyniard, who was only too glad to go, and Mounteagle, who would very much have liked to stay and hear what happened so that he could look after his own interests. But what the Lord Chamberlain had to say was for the ears of the King and Salisbury alone.

He found James pacing the Private Gallery, while Lord Salisbury sat at a desk working through a pile of state papers. In Scotland, James had grown up among plots from his childhood. It was not surprising that the King was nervous and had a horror of violence.

"Well, my Lord?" he asked impatiently.

"Sire, the cellar below the Parliament House is rented, as is Whyniard's small house next to it, to Thomas Percy, who as you know is cousin to the Earl of Northumberland, and does much business for him. Thomas Percy is an ardent Catholic and has the reputation of being a rash, violent man. There is a large quantity of wood stored in the vault under Parliament House, much more I think than Master Percy would need for two winters even if he lived all the time in Whyniard's house, which he does not, being as your Majesty knows always about his cousin."

"Ai, Ai," the King cried, plucking at his beard with a trembling hand. "This is sair news. My Lord, I am sure that there is gunpowder stored under all that wood."

"Thomas Percy's servant was in the vault when we went down there, and seemed to be trying to hide himself in a dark corner. He is a tall, desperate-looking fellow."

The King turned pale. "This will not do. This will not do at all, my Lord. You must have the vault searched thoroughly. Every log of wood must be turned; and let Whyniard's house be searched afterwards. It is my order. I will speak to the Earl of Northumberland about his cousin. But let there be as little stir as possible about the searching. If there is a Catholic plot, we do not want every Catholic in England in revolt to support or to rescue the plotters. We must take these men privily and find out who are behind them. You must arrest this servant, and the vault must be searched tonight. Where is Thomas Percy?"

"I believe he is at his lodging in London, Sire."

"There, you see," the King said quickly. "What does he want with a lodging, as well as with Whyniard's house? Why should he need so much fuel for the house when only his servant lives in it? I do not like that. I do not like it. And I remember how the Queen told me that this Thomas Percy has been coming into Prince Charles's nursery every day and bringing him toys and playing with him. The Prince's nurse spoke to the Queen about it. Now why should Thomas Percy do that? He has some design upon the Prince. Oh, we are in great danger from evil men! We must watch Thomas Percy closely. Meanwhile, my Lord, let the search be made tonight. To whom will you entrust it?"

"I thought, Sire, to send Sir Thomas Knyvet, who is a Justice of the Peace for Westminster and a very prompt and discreet servant of the Crown."

"Send him then, and a troop of soldiers with him. Let him go late tonight so that, if there is a plot, the conspirators will by that time think themselves safe and may the more easily be caught. And let me have word at once of what Knyvet finds."

The Lord Chamberlain kissed the King's hand and left him to go and send for Sir Thomas Knyvet.

Meanwhile, the conspirators did not feel as safe as the King imagined. Early in the evening, Guy Fawkes went round to Thomas Percy's lodging, where he also found Robin Catesby and Jack Wright. He told them about the Chamberlain's visit to the cellar.

"They will search again," Catesby said, " and find the gunpowder. We are finished there. We had better put all our strength into the uprising in the Midlands. Everard Digby waits for us at Rugby."

Guy Fawkes wondered if Catesby really supposed that an uprising which had been so sketchily prepared and which depended on the destruction of King, Lords and Commons would be likely to take place if those authorities were not destroyed.

But Tom Percy struck in. "We go too fast. They may not search again. They have seen the vault empty of anything except wood. Fools only see what is before their eyes. Let us not give up hope until the last moment. Let

Guy remain in Whyniard's house for tonight and hide himself in the cellar before tomorrow morning if the gunpowder is still undiscovered. Are you willing to do that, Guy?"

Guy Fawkes nodded. He would see the thing through to whatever might be the end. He went back to Whyniard's house.

Besides Catesby, Jack Wright and Tom Percy, four more of the conspirators, Ambrose Rookwood, Robert Keyes, Christopher Wright and Thomas Bates were still in London. So was Francis Tresham, but he did not come near the others. He had evidently decided to play no further part in the plot. He knew better than anyone that the King had been thoroughly warned and that the whole affair could only end in disaster.

Tom Percy, who was bold enough for anything, sat down to dinner that night with his cousin the Earl of Northumberland as though nothing unusual was happening. He even asked his cousin if there was any special news about the Opening of Parliament.

Chapter 15
Arrest

Through the long dark hours of the evening of November 4th, Guy Fawkes waited alone in Whyniard's house.

He did not mind being alone. He had never married, and never had close friends. Soldiering and the Catholic faith were the two things that really mattered to him. He was doing now what be believed to be a soldier's duty in the cause of his religion.

He thought is safer not to light a fire, nor even to burn a candle. Better that Whyniard's house should seem to be empty to anyone who might come to look. If they searched the vault again and found the gunpowder they were certain to come here, too. It was a very cold evening with a chill mist from the river. Guy Fawkes wrapped himself in his cloak and walked up and down to warm himself.

Every hour or so, he walked round to the Parliament House, unlocked the door of the cellar, and cautiously flashed his lantern light on the pile of fuel. Each time he saw, with relief, that nobody had touched it. He carried now inside his doublet the fuse and the slow match which he was going to use to light the gunpowder. If all went well the match should burn for fifteen minutes before setting off the gunpowder. Guy Fawkes would have fifteen minutes in which to save his own life. It should be enough for him to slip out of the vault and be halfway up the Strand before the explosion. But if he was discovered in the vault by searchers, as he might well be even at the last minute, he intended to put the match to the gunpowder at once, and blow himself up with those who came to capture him.

After his third expedition to the vault he went back to Whyniard's house to eat something. Then he began his steady pacing up and down again. He had no idea of the time. He listened to footsteps in the street. There were not many people about on this damp, foggy evening.

Once he heard footsteps come towards the door of Whyniard's house and stop. He stood still, a hand on the pistol in his belt. There was a knock at the door. It was a gentle knock; it did not sound like the thundering summons of a search party of soldiers.

Guy Fawkes decided to risk opening the door. He went quietly to it and slid the bolt back. He opened the door a little way, and peered out. A man who seemed to be alone was just visible in the dark.

"Guy. It is I, Robert Keyes."

Guy Fawkes opened the door wider. "Come in, Robert."

"No, I cannot stay. But Thomas Percy sent you his watch so that you might know the time." Robert Keyes disappeared into the night. Guy Fawkes bolted the door again, took the watch into a far corner of the room where no light could shine out of the window, lit his tinder box and looked at the time.

It was only ten o'clock. He had thought that it must be near midnight. He smiled grimly at his mistake. He had kept vigil often enough in a besieged town. He should have remembered how the hours drag. But he was very glad to have Percy's watch. It would be helpful to know how the

D

night was passing. His plan was to go round just before dawn and settle himself with his match and fuse in the vault. He would be able to hear the voices and footsteps of the Lords and Commons assembling overhead and he would know by the sound of trumpets when the King and Queen and the young Prince took their places.

It struck him that it might be sensible to get some sleep. He thought that he would walk up and down for another hour, then pay a last visit to the vault. If there were still no signs of a search, he would come back to Whyniard's house, and rest for an hour or two on his bed upstairs without taking off his doublet or his boots.

He began to walk up and down again. He guessed that it must be near midnight, and was taking out his tinder box again when he heard a faint sound from the street outside. It was not a footstep; it sounded like a clink of metal. He went to the door and listened. Now he heard footsteps, quiet footsteps as though several men were stealthily approaching the house.

Guy Fawkes waited a minute, expecting a knock. No one knocked. His instinct was always to go forward to meet danger, and the long wait had tried his nerves more than he realized. He opened the door and peered out into the dark.

His arms were seized and pinned to his sides. Men were all round him, pressing upon him, holding him. He tried to struggle but there were too many of them. A rope was flung round his arms, the knot was pulled tight.

A voice called out, "Have you trussed the fellow firmly? Then bring him with us to the Parliament House. Quick march."

By Tom Percy's watch it was just after midnight. The long-awaited day of November 5th had begun.

Chapter 16
The Second Search

Leaving four of the soldiers outside to guard Guy Fawkes, Sir Thomas Knyvet led the rest of his men into the vault below Parliament House, and ordered them to make a thorough search. Their lanterns flashed this way and that in the dark.

Sir Thomas pointed to the great pile of wooden logs. "See if there is anything under those."

As the men scattered the logs and threw aside the stone and iron bars, the round shapes of the barrels hidden beneath them began to appear.

"Bring one of those here to me. Open it."

A soldier rolled one of the barrels across to Sir Thomas. When they had prized it open he thrust his hand in, brought out a handful and sniffed. "Gunpowder. I thought so."

He turned to the sergeant. "Send one of your men to the barracks for a cart or two. Have these taken to the yard behind the barracks, and set a strong guard over them. Be careful. There is enough gunpowder here to blow up a regiment."

When all the barrels had been rolled out, Sir Thomas went outside to where the four men waited with Guy Fawkes bound between them.

"Search the prisoner."

The sergeant shone his lantern onto Guy Fawkes as two of the soldiers turned out his pockets and tore open his doublet. One of them found the slow match and the fuse hidden beneath it. He handed them to Sir Thomas.

"You had intended to use these to set off the gunpowder and blow up Parliament House, fellow?"

"If you had found me in the vault," Guy Fawkes replied, "I would have set a light to the powder at once and blown all of you up with me."

Sir Thomas, without troubling himself to answer, swung round on his heel.

"Bring him to the Palace."

The Earl of Salisbury and the Lord Chamberlain had been so anxious to know the result of the search that neither of them had gone to bed. When they heard that a store of gunpowder had been discovered in the vault, and that Percy's servant had been taken with a fuse and slow match hidden on him, they decided to rouse all those members of the King's Council who were sleeping in the Palace.

Everyone thought that there was urgent need for prompt action. They guessed that the plot to blow up the Parliament House must be part of a wider design. Who could tell what else the Catholics were planning for this day which had already begun. There might be an insurrection all over England! They decided, after consultation among themselves, to rouse the King and to bring the captured servant, John Johnson, before him.

At four o'clock in the morning, they led Guy Fawkes, bound, into the King's bedchamber. The servants, hastily roused from sleep, were blowing up the ashes of the fire and piling on more wood. The King, wrapped in a short fur-lined coat with an embroidered nightcap on his head, was sitting up in bed, propped by a heap of pillows.

The King looked yellow, fretful and nervous. His hands were trembling at the thought of the danger he had escaped by only a few hours, but his mind was alert. He had already given an order that the Opening of Parliament should be postponed for a few days. He looked on and listened with close attention as Salisbury questioned the prisoner.

"What is your name?"

"John Johnson, servant to Master Thomas Percy."

"You have been in charge of the vault below Parliament House, where we have discovered a great store of gunpowder hidden beneath firewood. Do you deny that your intention was to blow up the King, the Lords and the Commons at the Opening of Parliament.

"No," Guy Fawkes replied calmly. "That was my intention."

"Why did you intend this?"

"For one thing, I wanted to blow the beggarly Scots back to their native mountains."

There was a gasp of indignation from the assembled Councillors.

The King leaned forward and pointed a shaking forefinger at the captive. He said, like a nurse speaking to a naughty child, "Come now, are you not sorry for such a desperate purpose?"

"A desperate disease requires a desperate remedy," the prisoner replied.

Sir Thomas Knyvet came forward and handed a letter to Salisbury.

"The fellow says, my Lord, that his name is John Johnson, but we found in his pocket an opened letter from a gentlewoman addressed to 'Master Guy Fawkes'. He is no peaceful servant, he bears on his breast the scars of old wounds. It is likely that he has served in the foreign wars."

The King suddenly asked Guy Fawkes in French if this was true. As it was not worth while to lie about it, Guy Fawkes answered in French that he had been in the foreign wars.

They could get nothing else out of him. He would only repeat when questioned that his name was John Johnson, that he had intended to blow up Parliament House during the Opening, and that he did not repent of his intention. He would not say if anybody else knew what he was planning to do. He would not say if his master, Thomas Percy, had any hand in it. He would not give the names of any other conspirators. He seemed to be neither ashamed nor afraid. He let most of their questions go unanswered and confronted them with what appeared to be in-difference.

In the end the King ordered him to be taken to the

Tower. Sir Thomas Knyvet went with him to commit him to the care of the Lieutenant of the Tower, Sir William Wade.

It was still early but the King could not go to sleep again. His mind was too much disturbed by images of what might so easily have happened. He saw plainly enough that this man John Johnson or Guy Fawkes or whatever his name was, could not have been in this gunpowder plot alone. Who were the others and where were they? Who was behind them? What else were they planning, perhaps even for the day that was just dawning?

"This John Johnson," the King muttered to himself, "is all the clue we have. Except that he calls himself servant to Thomas Percy—but does Percy know anything of him or not? If we can only find out about this man it may lead to the discovery of the other conspirators."

Sitting up in bed and pulling down the fur-lined sleeves of his coat over his chilled wrists, the King called for his tablets. He wrote out a rough draft of a list of questions that should be asked of this John Johnson, or whoever he might be.

1. As to what he is. For I cannot hear of any man that knows him.
2. Where was he born? And when?
3. What were the names of his friends?
4. What is his age?
5. Where has he lived?
6. How has he lived, by what trade?
7. How did he receive the wounds in his breast?
8. If he was ever in service with any other before Percy?
9. How came he in Percy's service and when?

10. Why was the house held by Percy?
11. How soon after getting it, did he begin his devilish practices?
12. When did he learn to speak French?
13. What gentlewoman's letter was it that was found on him?
14. Why does she call him by another name?
15. If he was ever a priest?
16. When he was converted and by whom?

The King felt a little better. It seemed to him that by this list he had covered nearly everything. He sent the questions to the Lord Lieutenant of the Tower, with orders that if John Johnson could not or would not answer them, he was to be tortured to make him answer. "But," wrote James, "the gentler tortures to be used on him first." He ended the letter, "And so God speed you in your good work."

Chapter 17
Bonfire Night

By the middle of that cold winter's morning, a great many of the citizens of London knew that the Opening of Parliament was postponed because, at the last minute, a Catholic plot to blow up the King, Lords and Commons had been discovered.

Everybody was out in the streets, exchanging stories about it. Some said that a general Catholic Rising had been planned; that many other parts of the city would have been blown up; that thousands of honest citizens would have been burned in their beds; and that the Catholics had intended to burn down all the Protestant churches.

Of course, many people said, Spain was behind it, Spain who only seventeen years before had sent her great Armada with the blessing of the Pope of Rome to try and conquer England. Perhaps, some nervous citizens suggested, Spain was sending another Armada now! After all, the militia had been called out, which showed how immediate the danger was. Only those who could remember the year of the great Armada had seen so many steel breastplates and morions, or helmets, in the streets of London before. Yes, undoubtedly Spain was behind the plot.

A number of young men were so strongly convinced of this that they rushed off to the Spanish Embassy and with the help of the beggars and vagabonds who were always hanging about the streets, created a noisy demonstration in front of the barred gates. Then, feeling that they had done something useful to help to preserve their country and the Church of England, they scattered and went to the various taverns to talk about it all with their friends.

Ambrose Rookwood was the first of the conspirators in London to ask what he should do.

"I cannot help you," Percy said. "You had better shift for yourself . . . . as all of us must do."

When Rookwood left him, Percy called for his horse. As he mounted at the door of his lodging he said to his servant: "I am undone."

The servant, who had been with Percy for some time and knew all his rash ways, looked at him with dismay. "Why, what have you done, Sir, that you should say that?"

"Let it satisfy you that I have said so." Percy nodded grimly, and rode off as fast as he could through the crowded narrow streets.

Tom Winter heard so many different stories that he was not sure whether Guy Fawkes had managed to set a light to the gunpowder at the right time or not. He set out to walk to Parliament House, but was stopped by soldiers guarding the streets all round it.

But he could see that Parliament House was still standing. The plot had failed. Tom Winter turned back to his lodging in the Strand, mounted his horse and rode North. About the same time, Robert Keyes, Kit Wright and Ambrose Rookwood rode out of the city, spurring their horses until they were in a lather of sweat even on this cold November morning.

Near Dunstable they overtook Percy. They rode on together, throwing their cloaks into a hedge to lighten the weight for their horses, so that they could travel faster.

A few miles north of Dunstable, they met Robert
Catesby and Jack Wright, who were waiting for the first
news of the explosion before riding to summon the
Catholics of the Midlands to rise. They were hoping to see
Guy Fawkes who, if the slow match had as he expected
given him time to escape, should have been the first to
bring the news that the Parliament House had gone up into
the air.

Instead, Catesby and Jack Wright saw Ambrose Rookwood and Kit Wright on their panting horses. Rookwood
called out, "Guy Fawkes is taken and the plot discovered."

Catesby and Jack Wright waited to hear no more, but
rode hard after the other two. They were held back

because Catesby's horse cast a shoe, and he was obliged to stop and find a blacksmith to shoe him. This delayed them all, for although he urged the others to go on, they did not want to leave him too far behind. It was now pouring with rain and the tired horses slipped and stumbled on the muddy roads. It was evening before they arrived at the house of Catesby's mother, near Ashby St. Leger.

In London meanwhile, the only one of the conspirators besides Guy Fawkes who had come under suspicion was Tom Percy. He had rented Whyniard's house, and the vault under Parliament House; the mysterious John Johnson was his servant. A warrant was at once issued for Percy's arrest. It described him as "tall with a great hoary beard, a good face, hair mingled with white hairs but the hair more white than the beard. He stoopeth somewhat in his shoulders, is well coloured in the face, long footed and small legged."

The ostler at the tavern where Percy had lodged gave information that he had ridden off in a hurry that morning. But, whether out of good will to Percy or just because he had not been taking notice, the ostler said that he thought Percy had ridden towards the South. The King's Council at once sent messengers to all the Channel ports with orders to the Port Authorities to stop Percy, and the Constable of Gravesend travelled at full speed to Dover, where it seemed most likely that the fugitive might try to board a ship going to the Netherlands. Meanwhile, his cousin the Earl of Northumberland felt very uneasy on his own account, and made haste to assure the King and Salisbury that he had known nothing of any plot that his kinsman and agent was engaged in.

In London, on the evening of November 5th the bells of every Protestant church rang out a joyful peal. People staggered with armfuls of broken wood and rubbish to any open space, piled up bonfires and lit them. The Spanish Ambassador, who was only too eager to show, what was indeed the truth, that he had known nothing at all about the gunpowder plot, ordered an enormous bonfire to be lit in front of the Spanish Embassy and himself came out and scattered money among the crowd. There had not been such rejoicing in London since the defeat of the Spanish Armada. Then the news had come on a summer evening; on this cold night, anyone who could get near a heap of burning wood was not only eager to celebrate but glad to keep warm.

People sang psalms in the streets, and all those who could afford it feasted. It was not because they loved the Scottish King so much. After all, he had only been on the throne for two years. Besides, he did not, as Queen Elizabeth had done, enjoy showing himself to the people. He was afraid of them and they laughed at him, at his shambling movements, his dreary clothes, at the way his mouth was always open because his tongue was too large. No, the people did not love him and as Parliament had now been prorogued for a year and a half, they could not help feeling that they were no worse off without it. But they did feel, and those of them who were better at expressing themselves said, that King and Parliament were the chosen government of the British nation just as the Church of England was the chosen religion. It was not for a handful of men, probably, they thought, in the pay of foreigners, to destroy what England had chosen to set up for herself. Besides, what a horrible thing to use gunpowder to blow up the King and the Queen and the young Prince as well as so many lusty men who had wives and children of their own at home!

"Who were they then, these gunpowder plotters?" somebody shouted.

"All I know is that one was called John Johnson, or some say, Guy Fawkes."

"I should like to see this John Johnson or Guy Fawkes blown up himself."

"Let's burn him!" somebody yelled.

One of the many young apprentices who were dancing round the fires picked up a bundle of straw, rolled it in some rags and clapped his own hat on top of the bundle.

"Here's your Guy Fawkes!"

The crowd roared with delight as the makeshift figure caught fire and blazed up. They watched it until it was reduced to ashes.

One man wrote to a friend, "That night there were as many bonfires in London as the streets would permit."

Chapter 18
The End of the Plot

The Opening of Parliament was announced for Saturday, November 9th. During the preceding days, King James suffered from an attack of nerves. He would not go out of his private rooms in the Palace, nor dine, as his custom was, with the whole court. He would not see any visitors. He shrank even from the English Lords who made up his Council. Salisbury he had to admit, but except for him he would only have near him the Scottish Lords who had come with him from his own country. Everybody felt doubtful as to whether the King would find the courage to go and open Parliament when the day came.

Lord Hartington, who had charge of the young Princess Elizabeth, moved her from the country to the town of Coventry for her greater safety. They told her that the Catholics had been plotting to blow up her father and mother and brother and make her Queen. The little girl exclaimed in horror, "What sort of a Queen should I have been by this means? I would rather have been with my father in the Parliament House than wear the crown on such a condition!"

Meanwhile John Johnson was imprisoned in a narrow underground cell in the Tower. There was no light in the cell, it was damp and bitterly cold; it opened off the torture chamber.

On November 6th, the Lord Lieutenant of the Tower

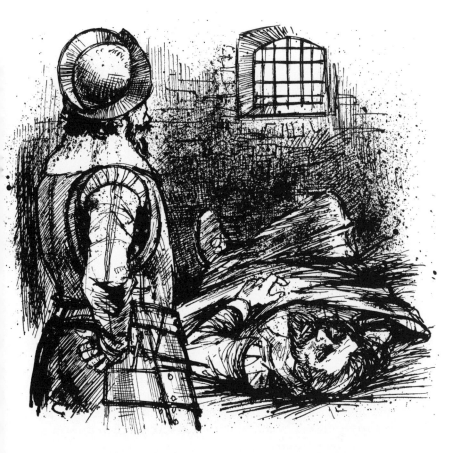

began to examine Johnson again, but got nothing from him. He refused to give his real name; he refused to give the names of his fellow conspirators. He would say nothing about the plot except that "giving warning to one overthrew us all."

On the next day, November 7th, he was tortured. He admitted that the plot had started eighteen months ago, and that there had been a plan to put Princess Elizabeth on the throne. He admitted that his real name was Guy Fawkes, and that he came from York. He would not give the names of any of his fellow conspirators.

That evening, when Guy Fawkes was resting after the torture, the Lord Lieutenant of the Tower had a long talk with him and believed that he was beginning to give way and that he would tell everything when he saw the rack and the other instruments of torture again the next morning.

But Guy Fawkes, bigoted, limited, and unscrupulous about murder, was an extremely brave man, and had a good soldier's loyalty to his comrades. Next day he again resisted torture. He was, the Lieutenant said, "in a most stubborn and perverse humour as dogged as if he were possessed."

Meanwhile, there was an order out for Tom Percy's arrest, and information about him and about the other conspirators was coming in to Lord Salisbury from different quarters. A servant of Sir Everard Digby went to a Justice of the Peace and told everything he knew. On November 7th, a Royal Proclamation was issued in London denouncing the rebellion, accusing "Thomas Percy, gentleman, and some other of his confederates," and urging all sheriffs and Justices of the Peace, Mayors, Bailiffs, Constables and other officers, to do their duty and capture the plotters.

By the evening of November 7th, all the conspirators except Guy Fawkes and Francis Tresham had reached Holbeach House, near Stourbridge in Worcestershire. The owner, Stephen Lyttleton, was a Catholic who had joined the hunting party arranged to capture Princess Elizabeth.

The Sheriff of Worcester, Sir Richard Walsh, had information that these conspirators and a handful of their supporters had reached Holbeach House. He sent for a larger party of soldiers, and kept a watch on the house until these soldiers could reach him.

110

Inside the house, the fugitives were in a miserable condition. They had ridden for two days through driving rain. They were soaked to the skin and tired out. They knew that their plot was a complete failure and that they had little chance of escape.

Some of the gunpowder which had been collected for the uprising was stored in Holbeach House. Lyttleton, looking at it that morning, had found it damp and had ordered it to be brought into the hall to dry. A heap of it piled up on a large dish had been placed not far from the fire where the conspirators were now huddled.

Robert Winter began to tell them about a dream he had had.

"Last night I saw all the churches of London standing crooked with their steeples awry. I saw the people inside the churches and they were people I knew, but they looked strange to me; their faces were all blackened with fire."

The dream did nothing to encourage the conspirators. They shivered and drew closer to the hearth while the steam went up from their wet clothes.

A servant came into the hall carrying an armful of logs. Nervous, like everyone else in the house, he threw the logs carelessly into the fire. A live coal flew out and landed on the dish of gunpowder.

There was an explosion that shook the room. When the smoke had cleared away there were cries of horror from the other conspirators, who saw that the faces of Catesby, Rookwood and Grant were scorched and blackened.

Robert Winter cried out, "My dream! The faces I saw in my dream! Depend upon it, the finger of Almighty God is here Heaven itself is against us and is punishing us with our lives."

Catesby was so shaken that he called out "Yes!"

Jack Wright shouted hysterically, "Let us set fire to the rest of the gunpowder and all go up together."

It seemed to the conspirators that God himself had spoken by turning their own dreadful weapon against them. From that time, none of them entertained any real hope of escape.

Catesby's servant, Thomas Bates, had a wife and children. He was already very sorry that his devotion to his master had led him into this disaster. He decided to go quietly away, on the chance that he might be forgotten or at least that he might see his wife and children again.

Kit Wright, happening to look out of the window of an upstairs room saw Bates going. He leaned out and dropped down a bag containing a hundred crowns.

"Give them," he called softly, "to your family."

When Kit Wright went down into the hall again he found his brother Jack with Stephen Lyttleton and Everard Digby standing up booted and spurred as for a journey. They were going to try and find another hiding place farther off. Catesby nodded good-bye to them with a half-scornful smile but when they had gone out he took his rosary in his hand and began to say his prayers. Rookwood did the same.

They were still praying when the door opened and Tom Winter came in. He sniffed the powder in the air and rubbed his eyes as the smoke tickled them.

He said to Catesby, "What do you mean to do?"

"We mean to die here," Catesby answered.

At eleven o'clock next morning the Sheriff of Worcester, who had by now been reinforced by a large party of soldiers, surrounded Holbeach House. He did not know how many men were there; he knew that since they had been preparing for an uprising they must have a good supply of arms and powder. He ordered the soldiers to approach cautiously, taking cover behind the bushes and firing on the doorways and windows.

The conspirators in the house did not see the troops until they were near and started firing. Tom Winter went out into the courtyard to look if a way of escape was open at the back of the house. He was immediately struck by a bullet in the shoulder.

Jack Wright and Ambrose Rookwood took up their positions in the door of the house to defend it. Both were shot and wounded.

Catesby moved to the doorway. "Stand by me, Tom," he said to Winter. "We will die together."

"I have lost the use of my right arm," Tom Winter said. "I fear that I shall be taken."

The Sheriff was anxious to take some of the conspirators alive and had had orders from London to bring in Tom Percy a prisoner. Salisbury wanted to find out, among other things, how much the Earl of Northumberland knew of his cousin's activities.

The Sheriff ordered his men to stop firing from a distance and move in to the attack.

The two Wrights were killed almost at once. Catesby and Tom Percy fought heroically; they had never been short of courage. The soldiers fired again at close range, and Catesby dropped dead. Tom Winter, who had fought gallantly with one arm, was wounded by a pike thrust in the stomach and taken prisoner. Tom Percy was badly wounded in several places. The Sheriff had no surgeon with his hastily assembled force. He gave orders that Percy should have his wounds treated as much as possible and be carried off to London in a litter. Percy, bandaged by careless hands, died in the litter on the way to London.

Rookwood, Tom Winter and Grant were taken to London and imprisoned in the Tower. Robert Keyes,

Digby, Thomas Bates and Francis Tresham were all captured during the next three days. Only Robert Winter was still free, wandering about the countryside.

The news of the death and capture of nearly all the conspirators encouraged the King and on November 9th he opened Parliament. He made a long speech thanking God that his life had so miraculously been preserved. Parliament House that day was a scene of great rejoicing.

In the Tower, Guy Fawkes was still being questioned daily under torture, and still refused to give the names of his fellow conspirators. But on November 9th he broke down on the rack and told about the meeting at the house near St. Clements Church and how Father Gerard had celebrated Mass, and four of them had taken the oath and the plot had started.

It was not until November 17th, when he had been daily stretched on the rack, that he gave the full story and the names of the men who by that time, except for Robert Winter, were dead or in prison. Guy Fawkes was so weak and faint that he could hardly sign his statement. He wrote "Guido," the name by which he had been known in the Spanish Army for so many years. He tried to add "Fawkes" but could only trace two feeble marks on the paper before he fainted.

The Sunday after the Opening of Parliament was proclaimed a day of National Thanksgiving. Bells rang again in all the churches, and special sermons were preached. At St. Paul's Cross in the yard that surrounded the old Cathedral the Bishop of Rochester preached on a text from the psalms. "Great Deliverances gave He to the King . . ." The Bishop announced to the congregation at the end of his sermon that half the conspirators had been killed in a fight at Holbeach House and the rest taken prisoner. God had protected the King, the Lords and Commons. The Gunpowder Plot was over.

Chapter 19
Trial and Punishment

On January 27th, 1606, the trial of the conspirators opened in Westminster Hall. Eight of them were still alive, Guy Fawkes, Tom Winter, John Grant, Everard Digby, Ambrose Rookwood, Thomas Bates, Robert Keyes and Robert Winter, who, after wandering wretchedly about the countryside, had been captured a few weeks earlier. Francis Tresham, who had also been arrested and imprisoned in the Tower, had died of an illness early in January.

All the prisoners had been imprisoned in dungeons in the Tower, but only Guy Fawkes had been tortured. His health was broken by the prolonged ordeal, and he was still weak and faint when they were carried down the river on a barge and brought before the Attorney General and the other lords.

The Attorney General, Sir Edward Coke, opened with a long violent speech. He dwelt on the brutal character of the plot.

"Miserable but sudden had their ends been who should have died in that fiery tempest and storm of gunpowder. But more miserable had they been that had escaped. And what horrible effects the blowing up of so much powder and stuff would have wrought, not only among men and beasts but even upon insensible creatures, Churches and houses, and all places near adjoining, you who have been martial men best know."

The prisoners, all except Sir Everard Digby, pleaded not guilty. Guy Fawkes, who spoke on behalf of the others, said that they had been accused of plotting what had never happened. They could not be punished for something they had never done. Guy Fawkes listened to much of the Attorney General's speech; it took all his strength to keep on his feet and to keep clear in his mind what he had agreed to say on behalf of them all. He himself had no hope except that the trial would soon be over. Rest for his racked body was all that he now cared about. But weak and shattered as he was, the others looked to him to speak for them.

They had no one else to do it; they were not allowed a lawyer to defend them. They had all been questioned in the Tower; in fear of torture they had answered truthfully. Their answers were now read aloud, and no further argument was needed to condemn them.

The Attorney General asked them, "What can you say wherefore a Judgement of Death should not be pronounced upon you?"

Thomas Winter said that he had brought his brother into the conspiracy. He begged that it might be considered enough if he was executed for both of them.

Robert Keyes asked for nothing. "Death," he said, "is as good now as another time, and for this cause rather than another." Robert Winter and Thomas Bates pleaded for mercy. John Grant said that he was guilty of planning a conspiracy but the plan had never been carried out.

Ambrose Rookwood pleaded that he had been drawn into the plot, "not from any malice to the King and the State, but for the faithful and dear affection that I bore to Mr. Catesby, my friend, whom I esteemed dearer than anything else in the world." He asked for mercy, "not that

I fear death but that a shameful death will leave a blot upon my name."

Sir Everard Digby also pleaded guilty. He said that he had been drawn into the plot by his affection for Catesby, and by his devotion to the Catholic religion. King James, he said angrily, had promised tolerance towards the Catholics, and had broken his promises.

The Earl of Salisbury, who was listening but had taken no part in the trial, rose to say that this statement was a lie, the King had never promised tolerance to the Catholics.

As the early winter night fell, and candles were lit in the Great Hall, the jury were sent out to decide upon their verdict. They came back in a very short time and announced that they found the prisoners guilty.

The Lord Chief Justice pronounced sentence of death on all of them.

Everard Digby turned to the assembled Lords. "If I may but hear any of your Lordships say you forgive me I shall go more cheerfully to the gallows."

Many voices from among the Lords cried, "May God forgive you as we do."

The prisoners were led out of Westminster Great Hall and down to the landing stage where the barge was waiting for them. They were hustled on board and the oarsmen rowed them swiftly along the great, dark river. As they saw the lights of houses on the banks, and the lanterns in the bows of passing wherries, they knew that this was the last time they would see them. They would only come out of the Tower to their execution.

On January 30th, Digby, Grant, Robert Winter and Thomas Bates were executed on a scaffold erected in St. Paul's Church Yard.

During the night the scaffold was moved to the Old Palace Yard in Westminster, very near to the Parliament

House. On January 31st, Guy Fawkes, Tom Winter, Ambrose Rookwood and Robert Keyes were executed. So great was the fury against them that soldiers, armed with halberds, had to guard the entrances to the yard to keep back the crowd.

They all prayed as their last moments came. Guy Fawkes said no word aloud, but was seen to be "Occupied with crossing himself and with idle ceremonies."

The bodies and heads of the conspirators were raised up on spikes above the gates of London, and on Parliament House as a warning to any other men who might think of upsetting the Government of England by violence.

A priest hunt began. Father Garnet, the Superior of the Order of Jesuit Priests in England, was captured and executed with two other priests.

As Father Garnet mounted the scaffold he said,"I pray God that Catholics may not fare worse for my sake."

They did fare much worse as a result of the Gunpowder Plot. King James had had a bad fright, and Salisbury took advantage of this to push through sterner laws against Catholics. They were forbidden to appear at court, or to live within ten miles of London unless they could prove that their work made it absolutely necessary. The work that they could do was limited; they could not become clerks, doctors or lawyers. They were not allowed to act as executors or trustees. They were prohibited from keeping any property that came to them by marriage if the marriage had been celebrated by a Catholic priest. Roman Catholics who had been educated outside England were declared outlaws.

As time went on, the laws against Catholics were not applied with the same severity, but it was not until the year 1829, in the reign of George IV that Catholics were allowed to sit in Parliament and to hold high office. It was no doubt partly the memory of the Gunpowder Plot that helped to keep the fear of Catholics alive for so long.

The memory of the plot has been kept alive in other ways. For over three hundred and fifty years, the boys and girls of England have celebrated the delivery of King and Parliament by lighting bonfires and burning effigies of Guy Fawkes on the evening of November 5th.